NAT NEWMAN
The Office of Dead Letters
a novella

LIVIDLILI

PRESS

First published by lividlili press 2021
Copyright © 2021 by Nat Newman

ISBN: 978-0-6452236-1-3

Contents

Prologue

There is no such thing as the Office of Dead Letters.

As anyone who has been to Basic School knows, the first rule of objectivity states that an object is either in transit or it is at rest. Sometimes, an object's resting place is not what you expect. Your house keys may not be hanging from their usual hook, but *they* are not lost. They are exactly where they are.

It is *you* who do not know where to find them.

An office which doesn't exist

T rudy and Marilyn didn't actually *work* in the small office on Mansfour Street in the City.

Although they could be regularly found in a room at the end of a linoleum-lined corridor, behind a frosted glass door, they most certainly did not have *jobs* there.

They just happened to meet in this room every weekday at 9am to sort through letters that hadn't yet arrived at their destination. They sliced through each envelope with their elegant blades, sorting them into piles, looking up their addresses, purely out of *zeal*. They were merely *interrupting* the objects in transit, and then giving them a nudge to get to the correct destination.

They had been doing this together for two years. But it was not a job. Nobody employed them. They had both retired, thank you very much, after the Last War. This was just a… hobby. An interest which took up a lot of their time.

After they had taken off their blazers and hung them on the rack by the door, Trudy set about making tea while Marilyn distributed their stacks of letters. Trudy made the tea strong and sweet with just a bit too much milk so that it slopped when she put the cup on Marilyn's desk.

"Oh, apologies," Trudy said, and wiped up the spill with the paper towel she had ready.

"Think nothing of it," said Marilyn, not even looking up from her methodical sorting of envelopes into their regions. Mini Atlas, Sucentral, Panko – each region with its unique identifier, all the way down to street level if you wanted to get particular. The zone codes of the Overworld Postal System were a marvel of modernity – although some people hinted that there may have been just a little Underworld magic in them, too.

Marilyn passed Trudy a pile of envelopes then sipped her tea.

"Lovely brew," she said. And they set to… Not to work. They set to zeal. Wielding their letter openers.

The heavy-faced clock that hung above the door tolled the quarter hour. The two women were already wrist deep in paper dust: white snow on Marilyn's black skin, smears of grey against Trudy's pale complexion. Their teacups sat at the sides of their desks, well out of the way of the falling debris.

Trudy picked up a new envelope. She read the address and went over to the row of shelves that lined the wall beneath the windows. Selecting one of the many directories, she returned to her desk and looked up the address. She slid the stainless-steel blade of her letter opener into a corner gap of the envelope, the fffft sound accompanied by a drizzle of dust falling as she sliced through the top. She put the blade down and quickly scanned the letter. Satisfied, she put it on a pile marked 'For Office of Found Letters'. These would be collected in the afternoon for redelivery.

Marilyn, at her own desk, had a similar neat pile of envelopes. Her letter opener was equally as sharp as Trudy's but had a comfortable leather grip. She performed the exact same actions as her colleague.

"Hm," she said, placing another envelope on the 'Found Letters' pile.

And so they passed the morning in a series of fffts and hms.

They paused regularly to moisturise their hands. They talked of stamps, of envelopes, of paper thickness, of anything except themselves. If Trudy had spent the weekend doing puzzles, Marilyn would never know. If Marilyn had cooked an excellent lobster bisque, Trudy couldn't even guess.

It was just the whirr of the clock, the pull of blade through paper, the flick of fingers through directory pages, the clatter of knife on desk, the swish, swish, swish of letters being exhumed from envelopes.

The clock struck the half hour. Trudy stood up, brandishing a letter in one outstretched hand, her letter opener in the other.

"Oh," she said.

The blade dropped from the air. Marilyn started back as it landed on Trudy's desk with a clatter.

"Hm," Marilyn said, staring at the empty space in front of her. Trudy and the letter had disappeared completely. Marilyn was alone in the non-existent Office of Dead Letters. She turned and looked at the clock. It was 9:31. It was finally time to go to work.

All that remained of Marilyn's officemate was a pink scarf hanging over the back of her chair, and a smear of matching lipstick on her teacup.

The last envelope Trudy had handled lay face-up on the desk where she had neatly placed it. Marilyn leaned over to read the address.

12 Jellicoe Street
CADENCE 12404

Marilyn examined the envelope which bore the OPS mark declaring it diverted. There were lots of reasons why that might happen: an incomplete address, a street that didn't agree with the suburb, a number that didn't belong on the street. It was the job of the Office of Found Letters to correct the destination address so the letter could complete its journey. The letter's diversion to the non-existent Office of Dead Letters was merely temporary.

The stamp on Trudy's last envelope was one that Marilyn recognised. It was from the mushroom collection, a really lovely set which had been released the autumn before last. So this stamp had been bought some time ago, or had been sold by a post office with leftover stock.

Putting aside the envelope, Marilyn fetched the directory that

Trudy had just consulted and looked up the address. A Miss Amber Jones lived at 10 Jellicoe Street, and Miss Felicity Aberystwyth at number 14. There was no entry where number 12 should be. That was odd, because even empty houses or lots had a listing. The efficiency of the Overworld Postal System relied on this fact. Marilyn placed a finger on the band of white space between 10 and 14, between Miss Jones and Miss Aberystwyth. She closed her eyes and concentrated on the gap. Yes. Sometime since this page had been printed, the listing for 12 Jellicoe Street had disappeared. The listings around it had knitted together, pulling closer. The very fabric of the page had changed.

Marilyn opened her eyes. An address had disappeared and so had Trudy. That meant only one thing.

Trudy had delivered the letter.

2

In the den of a skyscraper

The CEO of Megal Enterprises had a stunning corner office on the top floor of the newly opened Sky Tall Building. This extraordinary beacon of modern technology, its glass and steel facade towering eleven storeys above the City as tall as an Apple Tree, was visible for miles around. Its meaning was clear: Overworld had won the Last War and the geography was finally settled.

It was generally presumed that Mr Megal strutted around his aerie reading quarterly reports, yelling out memos, and keeping an eye on his myriad businesses. But just a few weeks after moving in to his lofty new office, Megal declared that he couldn't stand it. He told his personal secretary that he would sooner retire than stare at all that space, and so she had furnished a basement of the skyscraper with a den. To this cosy bunker, the recalcitrant CEO had retreated. Its collection of soft chairs and well-thumbed comic books brought him peace after all the tremors of the Last War, and so that is where he could be found most days.

He was safely ensconced in these – both the soft furnishings and the comics – when he was startled by the ding of the elevator.

"Miss Isabel," he said. "What a… surprise." His private secretary stepped out of the lift and gave a sniff.

"You're not answering my calls," she said. "But you're not dead. Although it smells like something is."

"I'm in perfect health," he said, ignoring the allusion to the den's cleanliness. He looked around at the mess, still holding his comic, but didn't get up. "I say. I can't think where I put my receiver."

Miss Isabel stepped gingerly into the breach and reached behind a sofa cushion. She fished out the receiver and handed it to him without a word.

"Thank you kindly," Megal said. He took the receiver and placed it on the sofa beside him, where it promptly slipped behind a cushion. "What was it that you wanted?"

"There's a woman here," Isabel said, using her chin to indicate the office upstairs. "Says it's about a letter."

"Oh my Two Worlds," Megal said, coming immediately to attention. "Is it Miss Marilyn?"

"That's right," Isabel said. "Black woman. Wearing Bentley's."

"I'll come right up," Megal said. "No, wait. Actually, bring her down here."

Isabel's eyes widened. Megal never did business in his den. "Yes sir," she said, and disappeared back in to the lift.

Mr Megal had just enough time to throw on a clean shirt and shove the room into a vague sort of order before the elevator returned and two women stepped out.

"Miss Marilyn," he said, feeling his neck begin to turn scarlet. "What a pleasure. It has been far too long."

He reached forward and held his hand out to her. She touched it with just the ends of her fingers, not removing her leather gloves. Mr Megal withdrew his hand with a cough and stepped back.

"As I recall," he said. "You're very fond of opening letters."

"I was up until this morning," Marilyn said. "But I'm afraid it has become rather lonely."

"Oh," Megal said. He took a few more steps back and sat on a puffy brown sofa. "Is that so?"

"Yes, I'm afraid it is."

Megal observed Marilyn where she stood by the lift. She hadn't taken off her hat and gloves, and she held her purse in front of her like a shield. Every hair was in place, every crease in her dark blue suit was perfect. She was so still. He could believe that her heart wasn't even beating.

"Forgive my rudeness," he said suddenly. "Please come sit down and tell me what happened." He indicated at his array of sofas and armchairs.

"Thank you, Mr Megal," said Marilyn. She stepped inside the circle of chairs and selected one that had a clear passage back to the lift. Megal repressed a smile; *typical enlistee*, he thought.

"My acquaintance, Miss Trudy, who, as you know, also loves to open letters—"

"Yes, I remember Miss Trudy," Megal said. "An excellent woman."

"Indeed. We were sitting in the room where we enjoy spending our days—"

Marilyn glanced over at the lift, where Isabel was still standing.

"Ah, please do go on, Miss Marilyn. Miss Isabel has my perfect confidence."

Marilyn nodded and continued. "We were sitting in the room where we go daily, when Miss Trudy opened a letter and disappeared."

Megal's eyes widened.

"It seems that she delivered the letter," said Marilyn, concluding her report.

Megal let out a long breath and sat back in his sofa. "I never thought it would actually happen."

"Nevertheless," said Marilyn, calmly taking the envelope from her purse. "It has."

Megal looked at the envelope in Marilyn's hand. She was very still and very upright. She sat there like a statue, looking completely oblivious to the world at the same time as seeming to pay close attention to everything all at once. He had the unnerving feeling that she could hear his thoughts, hear the sweat beading at his forehead, hear the beat of his heart, its increase in speed.

"Hm," said Marilyn.

"Ah," Megal said, remembering the envelope. He took it, peered at it and turned it about, but it was, in every conceivable way, a perfectly ordinary envelope. He looked inside. "But where did she go?"

"We can only assume she went to 12 Jellicoe Street," Marilyn said.

Megal snapped the envelope shut and leaned over to place it on the side table by Marilyn.

"Yes, of course," he said. "That seems most likely. As far as anything like this can be likely. And have you already ascertained... Does the address exist?"

"It is not in the OPS directory," Marilyn said. She paused. "Although I believe it used to be."

Megal whistled. "Dr Simon was right," he said, shaking his head. He pondered this thought for some time, as though it were more extraordinary than Trudy disappearing with the letter. He looked up suddenly.

"How much will you need?"

"Excuse me?" said Marilyn.

"How much money?"

"I'm sorry, sir, but for what?" She pulled back in her chair and drew herself even more erect.

"For the investigation."

"Oh," said Marilyn, relaxing slightly. "I had assumed that was Dr Simon's domain."

"Dr Simon has many excellent qualities, but his focus is primarily on the theoretical. I need someone practical to lead the investigation and find out what happened to Miss Trudy and locate her. I understand, Miss Marilyn, that you are a very practical woman."

Marilyn gave a slight nod.

"The Doctor will not be expecting you and he doesn't have a receiver," Megal said. "You'll have to go find him in the Apple

Quarter." He got up and went over to his desk, and took a cheque book from the top drawer.

"In that case," Marilyn said. "I'll need a car and a driver and $10,000."

"Excellent," he said. "Miss Isabel, kindly take the Cab and drive Miss Marilyn wherever she needs to go. Ensure my banker draws down this cheque for her immediately."

Megal paused as he was writing out the note. He looked up from his desk. "I'm terribly sorry," he said to Marilyn. "I don't recall your last name."

"Moon," she said. "Marilyn Moon."

"Miss Marilyn Moon," Megal repeated, then smiled, then blushed, then looked back down at the note and finished filling it out. Marilyn stood as he came over to hand it to her.

"Well, Miss Marilyn Moon, best of luck. I leave you in Miss Isabel's hands. I have complete faith in both of you."

"Thank you," Marilyn said. "I will not rest until I locate Miss Trudy." She reached out and shook his hand properly, although she still kept her gloves on.

3

Boulevards and warehouses

Marilyn could remember the years before the Last War, when the City had been Locale, before the geography had changed. Back then, the Apple Quarter had actually been full of the enormous fruit trees and dozens of apple processing plants. Mules would carry tonnes of apples into the warehouses every day to be cleaned and pickled, or ground into apple flour, or woven into apple silk, ready to be sent throughout the Two Worlds.

Those days were long gone. At the end of the Last War, most of the Apple trees had disappeared, except at the very edges of the region. New businesses had been invented and moved into the old spacious warehouses, capitalising on their proximity to the City. The Apple Quarter was now home to all sorts of curious organisations vying to make their way in the new geography of Overworld.

"It's so empty," Isabel said, as she drove them along the wide streets in Mr Megal's Cab.

"Hm," Marilyn said, clutching her hat. When she'd asked for a car, she'd expected one with a roof.

"It's such a… waste," Isabel said.

Marilyn glanced over at the young driver. Since the end of the

Last War there had been abundance in Overworld. Waste was not something that women like Isabel usually cared about.

But it was true; the Apple Quarter was vast. The boulevards were wider than a City block, built at a time when they were full of mules and wagons and workers of every description. The streets had to be this wide to ensure that none of the apple trees' roots touched one another underground. The trees had disappeared at the end of the Last War but the warehouses remained, looming large in the bare landscape, unaffected by the changed geography.

The Apple Quarter maintained some other quirks of its previous incarnation, namely that the warehouses appeared to be numbered at random.

"Were the numbers all jumbled up when the geography changed?" Isabel asked, after they had been driving around for 20 minutes, searching in vain.

"No," said Marilyn. "The numbers have never made sense. It's the history of the place. Underworld maths, perhaps."

Isabel shivered, but said nothing.

To add to the confusion, the warehouses were all identical wooden structures, except for a few that had been modernised with the addition of glass or steel. But for the most part, the two women drove through a silent forest of buildings.

The wide roads were the domain of a few omnibuses, transporting forlorn faces looking out of dirty windows. There were precious few people to be seen on the streets at this hour; they were all inside, working, working, working.

Is this what we fought for? Marilyn thought, not for the first time.

Isabel turned at an intersection and suddenly they could see one of the enormous apple trees directly ahead of them, its branches reaching to either end of the block and its crown as high as Megal's Sky Tall building. Isabel inhaled sharply and covered the brake, before quickly regaining her composure and carrying on.

"Never seen an apple tree before?" Marilyn asked.

"I heard they were big, but I didn't realise what big meant," Isabel said. "I mean, that's big."

"Yes, it's quite large," Marilyn said. She had seen her first apple tree as a child. Had even climbed one, once, although only as far as the second branch. Any higher and she would've had to wear a parachute.

"But I thought they were all gone. Why is it here?" Isabel said. Her eyes kept seeking out the top of the tree as she drove slowly along the road. "Is that the Orchard?"

Marilyn nodded.

"The edge of the Worlds," Isabel said.

"Nobody knows for sure," Marilyn said. "The Orchard could be part of Overworld."

"I wouldn't want to find out," Isabel said, and she tore her gaze from the tree and focused again on the road.

"There's number 44," Marilyn said, indicating the very last warehouse on the left. They were close to the tree and the Orchard now and she hoped her new companion would be tougher than she looked. Mr Megal had trusted her, but then, he was a businessman, not a soldier.

Isabel pulled the car over to the side of the road and Marilyn undid her belt.

"Let me just fix myself up," Isabel said, pulling out her compact. "I love the Cab but the wind dries my skin out. Probably not a problem you have."

Marilyn turned to look at the girl. She was young, and had proved garrulous on the drive out of the City. But was the secretary now being impertinent?

"You've got such great skin," Isabel went on. "Because, you know…"

Marilyn could tell the young woman was dying to say it, the phrase. She stared at her expectantly while Isabel powdered her skin.

"Right, let's go," Isabel said, snapping shut her compact and giving Marilyn a broad smile.

"Hm," Marilyn said.

The two women walked up the drive, their shoes crunching in the gravel. The sound reverberated off the wooden frame of the warehouse, but Marilyn heard nothing odd in it. The next nearest warehouse was to their left, but it looked dismally empty and very, very far away.

Marilyn was surprised to realise that Isabel was quiet; she seemed to be concentrating. She had taken her hat off and was fanning her face as she walked carefully but confidently on the uneven ground.

"Bentley's?" said Marilyn, pointing down to Isabel's shoes.

Isabel nodded and placed her straw hat back on her head. "Our doctor is not very welcoming," she said.

"Were you expecting an open front door?"

"I was expecting a door of any description."

Marilyn actually smiled. The girl had guts. She looked prim in her lemon-yellow dress and white gloves, and she had been awed by the apple tree, but she most definitely wasn't afraid.

"I can't smell a damn thing except that apple tree," Isabel said. She had taken off her hat again and seemed to be trying to catch the breeze. "Can you?"

Marilyn gave a sniff. "Nothing out of the ordinary," she said.

"Oh," said Isabel, leaning forward. "And paper dust. Quite a lot of paper dust."

"Hm," Marilyn said, looking down at Isabel's cheeky grin. She looked far too young, but somehow or other Isabel *had* been an enlistee, of that Marilyn was now certain.

Suddenly in the silence, they heard a scream and a wood panel of the warehouse thrust outwards. A man tumbled out, waving around a cigar.

"You little fucker!" he yelled out.

Marilyn and Isabel exchanged a swift look. "Dr Simon," Marilyn said, stepping forward. "How do you do?"

He whirled around in surprise. "What the devil?" he said.

Isabel approached and stood by Marilyn.

"My worlds!" Simon said, looking between them wildly. "There's two of you!" The smoke from his cigar was forming a purple haze around them.

"I'm Miss Isabel. We met before at Mr Megal's office."

"Yes," the Doctor said, after a pause. "Yes, I remember you. And you. You're from the experiment. Has something happened?"

"Perhaps, Dr Simon, we could go in," Marilyn said.

"And we'd appreciate it if you would leave the explosive outside," Isabel said.

Dr Simon looked at the cigar in his hand. "Fuck me!" he said. With more alacrity than Marilyn would ever have given him credit for, he hurled the thing into the empty field behind the warehouse where it exploded with an enormous bang, showering the air with tiny burning embers of deepest orange.

4

A lesson in physics

The interior of the warehouse belied its shabby exterior, offering scrubbed white walls, stainless steel tables, and a brushed concrete floor which was obviously swept and cleaned regularly. A few sooty marks showed where explosions had occurred, but otherwise it was a spacious and modern laboratory.

"So Miss Trudy has delivered a dead letter!" said Dr Simon, after Marilyn had given him a precis of the morning. He was washing his hands at a lab bench that had been converted into a kind of makeshift kitchen.

"Did you expect this?" said Marilyn. She and Isabel were sitting on stools on the other side of the bench.

"Well, no, not like this. I thought a letter could get delivered, but not the person holding the letter."

"Is she safe?"

Dr Simon went very still.

"Oh," he said. "I uh… I'm not uh…"

"You don't know where Miss Trudy is?" said Marilyn.

"Oh we know that! We know exactly where she is. She's at 12 Jellicoe Street," Dr Simon said. He wiped his hands dry on his trousers and leaned his elbows on the bench. "The problem is, we don't know where that is." He gave a short bark of a laugh.

"Hm," Marilyn said, and Dr Simon felt all the force of that little syllable. "I have been working in the Office of Dead Letters for the past two years, although that is the first time I have ever said that out loud. My colleague, Miss Trudy, has now gone missing. Miss Isabel and I have been charged with finding her. This was your experiment, Dr Simon. What information can you actually provide?"

"Wait," said Isabel, putting up her hand. "Do you mind if we start at the beginning? Like, why are we so excited about the post? What's a dead letter?"

"A way to seek out the impossible!" Dr Simon said.

"Oh… kay?" said Isabel.

Dr Simon collected himself. "In order to find the impossible, we had to create a place that didn't exist. The Overworld Postal System is the most efficient and accurate organisation in the whole of the Two Worlds. We used it to try to find the places that don't exist. The places that ought to exist, but have been swallowed up."

Isabel crinkled her eyes.

"He means parallel universes," Marilyn said.

"What is the first rule of objectivity?" said Dr Simon.

"An object is either in transit or at rest," Isabel said automatically.

"Excellent," said the doctor. "And if the object is interrupted whilst it is in transit?"

"Well, it would take the interruption as its new resting place."

"Unless it's a letter!" said Dr Simon, as if that explained everything.

Isabel blinked at him a few times. "Miss Marilyn?" she said, turning to her.

"An object always knows where it is," Marilyn said. "That's the most fundamental law in physics. Now, a letter knows where it has started, and it knows it is in transit. But what if its destination doesn't exist?"

"It goes to the OPS Office of Found Letters," said Isabel.

"This is the good bit," said Dr Simon. "We divert the letters! The OPS keeps the letters in transit and sends them to us!"

"To the experiment, yes," said Marilyn.

"But why?"

"Because when a letter is interrupted, it is both in transit and at rest," said Marilyn.

"The superposition theory?" Isabel said.

Dr Simon nodded. "When a letter is in superposition, it becomes aware of everything; its origin, its progress and its destination. Now, if a letter becomes aware of its progress and realises that it could never be delivered by the OPS, *it attempts to deliver itself*."

"But how?"

"That part we don't exactly know."

"There may be a bit of Underworld physics involved," Marilyn said.

"Indeed," said Dr Simon. "But we theorise that it must find its own way to its destination. If we can follow it, we can find places that exist, but not in the Two Worlds."

"Surely two worlds is enough," said Isabel. "Why would you want to find any more?"

"Because they would allow us to travel through all of time and space."

"Okay, let me get this straight," said Isabel. She stood up and began to pace around. "12 Jellicoe Street. It doesn't exist in our universe. If it had, the letter would have known its interruption was temporary and allowed itself to be delivered properly by the OPS. But through this *interruption*, it becomes aware that it can never be delivered."

"Yes," said Marilyn. "Knowing that its destination actually exists, but that nobody in this universe could find it, it uses any means possible to get there itself."

"So if 12 Jellicoe Street doesn't exist in Overworld, where exactly is it? Is it in Underworld?"

"No, no. It's not in the Two Worlds at all. It has been

swallowed," said Dr Simon. "By an anomaly, by a parallel universe, by another world."

"It sounds like you don't know where it is at all," said Isabel.

"Precisely!" said Dr Simon.

Isabel returned to her stool and perched at the edge of her seat.

"So you sit in here all day writing letters?"

"No, no," said the Doctor. "I have no idea who sent that letter. In order to work, it has to be a real letter written by a real person who really believed in the destination."

"Have you seriously been waiting around hoping that a letter would be addressed to a parallel universe and deliver itself?" Isabel said. "But the odds must have been astronomical."

"They were rather large, yes," said the doctor.

Marilyn stood. "We must begin. Miss Isabel, you now know as much as I do and the Doctor can tell us anything else on our way."

"On our way where?" he said.

"To Jellicoe Street, of course," said Marilyn.

5

A tale of two Tees

Isabel looked up Jellicoe Street in the glove box directory and set off confidently back toward the City. Dr Simon was riding in the back of the Cab, occasionally yelling out remarks such as "whee!" or "she really goes, doesn't she?"

"First time in a Cab, doc?" Isabel called back.

"First time in a car!" he said. "Knocks the pants off an omnibus!"

As they approached the city, Isabel took the detour around the east side. They passed through a few dismal suburbs before reaching the Cadence high street. A few moments later Isabel turned in to Jellicoe Street and stopped in front of number 10.

Dr Simon leaped over the side to get out of the car. He turned to the ladies as they got out using the actual doors.

"Let's go!" he said.

They stood at the fence between 10 and 14 Jellicoe Street; there was definitely no number 12. There was no empty lot, nothing to indicate that number 12 had ever existed. Just the fact of its non-existence. It was like the way things had disappeared when the geography changed, although Cadence had been untouched by the war.

The two houses at 10 and 14 were fairly similar. Just normal wide suburban houses on old-fashioned quarter-acre blocks, designed for commuters with families, probably built at the end of the Last War But One. They were part concrete and part Fibwood, the fake wooden slats starting to fray at the edges where they were exposed to the elements. The house on the left was painted blue, the one on the right a kind of cream. In short, they were wholly unremarkable.

Dr Simon stared all about him, took a step forward, stopped, stared around again and then turned to look at the two ladies with wide eyes. Marilyn realised with a sinking heart that he would not be leading the investigation.

"Let's do some recon to start," Isabel said, evidently feeling the same thing.

The fence between the two houses started some two metres from the curb. The lawn either side was the same length, suggesting that the owners mowed on roughly the same day. There was no shimmering in the air or any visual clue that a universe was hidden here. And yet, the air was too still, the street too quiet. There was definitely something unsettling about Jellicoe Street.

The doctor reached out to touch the fence, but Marilyn stopped him with one hand upon his shoulder. He looked at the hand and felt keenly its potential power.

"Let's question the neighbours first," Isabel said, placing her hand on his other shoulder.

"Capital idea," Dr Simon said.

They went first to number 10, the house on the left. They could hear the sound of a hoover in the front room and Isabel peered in the window as Marilyn rang the doorbell.

The woman who answered the door opened it only partway, careful not to let them see into the hallway beyond. It was a classic suburban defensive posture, Marilyn thought. Ready to slam the door in the face of anyone who tried to sell her a plan for a receiver.

"Yeah?" the woman said, her voice cautious. She took in Marilyn's neat skirt suit, her hat and gloves. "Look, if it's about religion, I'm not interested."

"Definitely not about religion!" Dr Simon said, a hint of offence in his tone.

"We just have some questions about your neighbours," Marilyn said.

"The neighbours?" the woman said. She opened the door a little further to peer out at them, and they could see that she was still in her pyjamas, a few old coffee stains down the front. "Not cops, but?"

"No," said Dr Simon. "Scientists."

This made the woman laugh. "Ha! Worse than religion," she said.

"I say!"

Without turning to look at him, Marilyn gently touched the back of Dr Simon's hand with one ungloved finger, and he was suddenly struck mute.

The woman stepped out on to the porch and pulled the front door shut behind her, leaning against it. "Well, what do you want to know?"

In the daylight of the porch, the woman was noticeably odd looking. Her hair was uneven and seemed to be several shades at once. Her mouth was neither a frown nor a smile, her nose twisted slightly. And her right eye was brown, the left one blue.

"Allow me to introduce myself. My name is Miss Marilyn, this is Miss Isabel, and the gentleman scientist is Dr Simon." Marilyn paused and waited.

"I'm Miss Tee," the woman said, eventually.

"Have you noticed anything unusual about your fence or the area where your two yards meet?" Marilyn said, pointing towards number 14.

There was a long silence as Tee looked at them all closely.

"The nerd's a scientist," she said. "But you two…" Her empty sentence said it all; City slickers, hoity toity ladies, *enlistees*.

Isabel stepped forward. "Miss Tee, please. This isn't bullshit. That fence. Is there anything weird about it?"

Tee looked at Isabel like someone was finally speaking her language. She glanced over towards the fence and shrugged.

"Looks normal to me."

"And what about number 12?" said Marilyn.

"Number 12?"

"Yes. You're number 10 and next door is number 14. So where's number 12?"

Tee shrugged. "Dunno."

"Maybe your land is part of number 12?"

"I never thought about it, to be honest. Could be."

"And has it never occurred to you before that there should be a number 12?"

"Not really," Tee said. "Do *you* think there should be?"

"What about unexplained movements," Marilyn pushed on. The Doctor, mute by her side, stared at her. "Things appearing or disappearing. Things you left in one place turning up somewhere else?"

"Not really. I mean, the bitch across the road still has my ladder."

"All right then," Marilyn said. She thanked Miss Tee for her time and the trio descended to the yard.

"Watch out for that one," Tee called out after them as they walked across to number 14. "She can be cranky."

As the trio made their way across the lawn to number 14, Dr Simon seemed to become unmute.

"What in the Two Worlds was that?" he said to Marilyn. "You asked all the questions I had in my mind! How did you know?"

"I only asked the obvious, Dr Simon," Marilyn said.

Isabel knocked several times before they heard the sound of movement. The woman who answered the door was remarkably similar to the woman at number 10, so much so that Marilyn, Isabel and Simon all looked at her, then looked over at her neighbour's house, then looked back to the woman in front of them. The same odd hair, the same asymmetrical face. She even had one brown and one blue eye, exactly mirroring Tee from 10.

"Who are you lot then?"

It was Marilyn who regained her composure first.

"Hello," she said. "We're in the area checking on scientific phenomena. Is this your house?"

"Youse woke me up to ask if this was my house?" she asked. "Of course it's me fucking house!"

"I say!" said Dr Simon.

"Quite right," said Isabel. "And a beautiful house, too. I particularly like this colour. Garlic powder, is it?"

The woman grunted.

"Horseradish," she said.

"Ah, of course," said Isabel. "I was tossing up between garlic and onion for my living room. I hadn't thought of horseradish."

"Was that all you wanted? To know the colour of me house?"

"That fence." Marilyn didn't point to the fence between 10 and 14 but the one on the other side, the one adjoining 16. "Is that your garden?"

"Look, I told the idiot from the City that those flowers are only a little bit poisonous. And anyway, if that stupid dog comes onto my property, that's his own fucking problem. Do you know how many times it has shat on my lawn?"

"It's a lovely garden," Marilyn said placidly. "Are you going to continue it on to the other fence?"

"The back, you mean?"

"The fence with number 10."

The woman tried to peer to her right, to where Marilyn was pointing, but didn't seem to be able to turn her head completely.

"Or perhaps the fence with number 12?" Marilyn said.

The woman still strained but seemed unable to move her head properly.

"What fence with number ten? There isn't no number 12."

"I'm sorry," Marilyn said. "I must be mistaken. I thought you had neighbours at 12. But there's only Miss Tee at number ten."

"Who? At number what?"

Marilyn didn't skip a beat.

"Your neighbour at number 16. I've forgotten his name. The one with the dog?"

"That bastard. Keefer is his name."

"Mr Keefer?" The woman was clearly uncouth, but Marilyn was momentarily checked by her blatant disregard for the honorific.

"Nah, the dog. The dog is Keefer. The owner is Mr Duncan. Both of them not worth anything. But you tell them that the flowers stay. They're on MY property."

"Yes, of course," said Marilyn. "You're absolutely in the right, Miss. I'm sorry, I've forgotten your name."

"The name's Tee," the woman said. "Like the drink. But more bitter. Ha!"

Marilyn smiled. "Thanks again, Miss Tee. We'll make sure there's no more bother with the City."

Tee stared at them as they set off down the porch, but the moment they were down the stairs, she slammed the door.

"Well, that was a complete waste of time," said Dr Simon, as they stood again by the fence. "I should have just left the people stuff to you while I began my measurements."

Isabel laughed, a nice long musical tinkle.

"But we know exactly where your fold in space is," she said.

"We do?"

"Of course we do," said Marilyn. "Miss Tee at 10 was aware of the fence and of the possible existence of number 14."

"But Miss Tee at 14 couldn't be made aware of number 10 at all," Isabel continued.

"She can't perceive the anomaly, yes," said the doctor. "But we already know where it is! It's between the two houses."

"Not quite, doc," said Isabel. She took a piece of paper out of her purse and drew two vertical lines on it. She wrote the numbers 10, 12 and 14, representing the houses.

10 | 12 | 14

She then drew a circle which enclosed 12 and the line between 12 and 14.

"Your anomaly, or fold, or whatever, has encompassed 12 Jellicoe Street," said Isabel. "But not just the house. As you can see, there's only one fence between 10 and 14, not two. So which fence has been absorbed by your anomaly?"

"Wait," said Dr Simon, turning to look towards number 10. "So the fence that is facing us right now isn't the fence between 12 and 14? It's actually the one between 10 and 12?"

The two ladies nodded.

"And in fact," Isabel said. "The side of the fence we can see right now belongs to number 12 Jellicoe Street. It's all that currently remains of that property."

Dr Simon looked about him with excited eyes. "So this is the exact spot. Not just between the two houses, but right here between that fence and number 14? Ladies! We're standing right on top of a fucking anomaly!"

"I say, Doc," said Isabel, but she was smiling.

6

Taking measurements

The trio standing in the side yard of number 14 Jellicoe Street was, assuredly, odd looking. Two well-dressed women seemed to be searching for a dropped glove or coin, while a tall, dishevelled man waved a curious instrument at the fence.

Across the way, at number 13, someone watched them through a partly drawn curtain.

Dr Simon was taking measurements with his device, while Marilyn and Isabel were looking for physical clues, something that might indicate the existence of number 12, or Trudy, or – wonder of wonders – perhaps the entry to whatever this anomaly was. Isabel was sniffing the air at various spots, once even getting down on to her hands and knees to smell the ground. Marilyn had taken off her gloves and was walking slowly up and down, her hands brushing against the fence.

Dr Simon's device gave out quiet beeping noises which seemed to Marilyn's ears to be noncommittal and uninformative. He was engrossed in the data he was receiving from the screen, and occasionally he would pause to look more closely.

It had been quite the morning, Marilyn thought. She had had

no idea, when she donned her suit and walked down to the Office of Dead Letters, that she would end up in Cadence with a secretary sniffing the ground and a doctor waving a stick at a fence. She had seen a lot of strange things during the Last War, most noticeably the changing of the geography, but this may have just taken the peculiar cake. She almost smiled. Almost.

She wondered what a parallel universe felt or looked or sounded like. How would they actually know if they found it? She suspected that Dr Simon didn't know and they were all working on instinct. It was not the ideal way to run an operation, but it was all they had right now. She only hoped that Miss Trudy would be found and could be extracted. She stepped past Isabel, who was sniffing a fence beam, and she stopped.

"What was that all about?" Marilyn said quietly. "The colour of the house?"

Isabel smiled. "Like I said, I'm repainting my living room."

"Sh…" said Dr Simon. "This is rather more important than interior decorating, ladies."

Marilyn threw the gentleman a little side eye.

"And what was it really?" she asked Isabel again.

"Aha," said Dr Simon. "I think…" He paused, then stood up straight and looked more carefully at the screen, shading it with one hand. "I think there is definitely some sort of possible anomaly potentially within the vicinity of this space just here."

"Would you like to add a few more qualifiers, doc?" said Isabel.

"It's just… It's just…"

"Dr Simon," said Marilyn. "Is your device actually able to detect anomalies?"

"Well, in a general sort of way. But it needs a little work," he said. "The algorithm I've programmed the ethometer with, I haven't quite refined it yet."

Marilyn sighed. "That is what you said two years ago when we began this project."

"I thought I would have fine-tuned it by now. It's not an easy thing to do, you know. This is very complicated mathematics. It's not bloody house paint."

"I understand," said Marilyn. "You thought you had longer. But the fact is, you don't. There's something odd here and we need to know exactly what it is so that we can recover Miss Trudy. Do you think it is actually possible to 'fine tune' this instrument to allow us to enter the anomaly?"

"Enter it?" said Dr Simon. "I never thought to enter it, only to measure it, to learn from it! I'm no explorer."

"How are we meant to recover Miss Trudy if we don't enter the anomaly?" Marilyn said, lifting her eyebrows.

Dr Simon was silent a moment. He stared at the ethometer. "It all depends on how much time we have," he said at last. "And that we don't know."

"Why not?" said Isabel.

"Well, anomalies exist in time and space. And we don't know how long this anomaly that Miss Trudy is in will last. If I had just one dimension to work with, its size or its duration or anything at all, I could extrapolate the rest."

"Is it possible that if the anomaly stops existing in time, Miss Trudy will return to our time and space?" asked Isabel.

"All of this is theoretical," said Dr Simon warily. "No one was supposed to enter the anomaly. I didn't know the letter would take whoever was holding it with it. I just thought it would be a piece of paper. At worst, a gift, a box of chocolates." He sighed.

"I will remind you, doctor, that this is *your* project," said Marilyn. "Miss Trudy and I were working on *your* project."

"Yes, yes, I understand."

"So what do you think we should do next?"

Dr Simon stared glumly at the screen of his device. He'd had two years – and now he couldn't think what he'd done with that time.

"FFF8E7," Isabel said.

"What's that?" Marilyn said.

Isabel took a step closer to Dr Simon. "FFF8E7," she said again. He looked up at her.

"Is that a code?" he asked. "I'm sorry. Cryptography was never my thing. I'm just a physicist."

"Eff. Eff. Eff. Eight. Eee. Seven," Isabel said, enunciating each letter and looking over at the beige wall of the house at number 16.

And he saw it then. He saw it behind her. The colour of the house.

"Cosmic latte!" he said. "The colour of the house. It's the average colour of the universe. But that's impossible. It's a theoretical colour. It's not reproducible."

"I'm telling you, doc," Isabel said. "I can see it with my own very good eyes."

"But to show the average of the universe, you'd have to have the whole of the universe."

"Not my field, Doc. I'm just telling you what I can see."

"That means… That means… The anomaly is finite on the outside but infinite on the inside."

"Can you work with that? Is that a dimension you can add to your maths?"

"Possibly," said the doctor. "Yes! Yes, I think it can help!"

"People have their uses, doctor," said Isabel. "When your instruments fail you, we need to rely on people."

"But she said it was horseradish!" the doctor objected.

7

A whiteboard and the stars

I t was obvious that they couldn't achieve anything else by exploring Jellicoe Street. Isabel could smell nothing unusual and Marilyn hadn't been able to feel anything out of the ordinary, except the general weirdness of the place that they could all sense. They drove back to Dr Simon's warehouse in the Apple Quarter.

Back in his own domain, Dr Simon began to prepare tea and toast, while Marilyn and Isabel pulled a couple of stools around a whiteboard. Isabel womanned the stand, wielding her marker like a conductor.

"What do we know so far?" she said, using her wand to elicit a response from the pit.

"Miss Trudy Grayling disappeared from the Office of Dead Letters at 9:31 this morning," Marilyn began. "She is missing, presumed to have delivered a letter to 12 Jellicoe Street, which does not currently exist in the Two Worlds."

Isabel made notes on the whiteboard and then added her own observations.

"The houses surrounding the presumed fold in space and time

are tenanted by two women with the same name who look remarkably similar."

"That was my favourite part," said Dr Simon, bringing over a pot of tea and setting it on a bench.

Isabel continued. "The first neighbour, who we will call T1 for short, was aware of her neighbour T2. The second neighbour, however, seemed unable to perceive anything to the anomaly side of her house."

"We believe that the anomaly is limited in space by the fence at number 10 on one side, and the nearest wall of the house at number 14 on the other," Marilyn said. "Although Dr Simon's instruments were not conclusive on this matter."

"No," said Dr Simon. He wiped his hands over his face as if he wanted to smooth his skin back. He did this several times and then tucked a rogue curl behind his ear.

"But you ladies were absolutely right. Where my instruments failed, we found out a lot from talking to the people. I believe T1 and T2 are mirrors of each other."

"Is the anomaly a reflective surface?" Marilyn asked.

"No, not like that," said Dr Simon. He had taken a piece of toast and he was holding his hand over his mouth while he spoke so he was a little muffled. "Like folds," he said.

"Foals?" said Isabel. "Baby horses?"

"Folds. Folds," Dr Simon said, more loudly, a few crumbs ejecting from his lips. "The valleys on either side of a fold. They mirror each other. They've been brought too close."

He swallowed his toast in a gulp, then took a pinch of his own shirt to demonstrate. Marilyn saw immediately.

"Of course, when you fold something, you're bringing together two parts that used to be separate."

Dr Simon nodded and took another piece of toast.

"But is it an anomaly or a fold?" Marilyn asked. "And what does this mean for Miss Trudy? What exactly is she in?"

"Miss Trudy is absolutely inside the anomaly," Dr Simon said. "The fold is something else. It's the external effect of the anomaly on our plane. The anomaly has folded the space time around it.

Like the text in the directory you looked at, Miss Marilyn. Space has condensed slightly around that area, brought two parts together, to compensate for the missing house."

Isabel added this information to the white board.

"And what of the neighbours?" Marilyn asked. "They had names. Miss Amber Jones and Miss Felicity Aberystwyth. Are they in the anomaly, too?"

"They have obviously been affected by the fold created by the anomaly," said Dr Simon. "The same way the colour of the wall was changed. I'm not sure… It may be irreversible."

They were all quiet for a moment, Marilyn thinking how often the civilian cost of life was rarely worth the battle. She hoped that she was wrong this time and the residents of 10 and 14 Jellicoe Street weren't lost forever, let alone whoever had lived at number 12.

"But what of the colour?" said Isabel. "I've never seen Cosmic Latte in real life, but I am certain that's what it was. You said that means the anomaly is infinite? What does that actually mean?"

Dr Simon had just shoved a freshly buttered piece of toast into his mouth and he shook his head.

"The inside of the anomaly is everywhere," Marilyn said, while the Doctor wiped a streak of butter from his chin. "In all of time and space."

Dr Simon nodded at her vigorously. "Indeed," he said. "Wherever Miss Trudy is, it is infinite. She herself may be spread out through the entire universe. Or she may be a tiny microscopic dot in an infinitely large space."

Marilyn stood abruptly and walked to the far wall where they had first come in. Reaching it, she did an about-face, walked briskly back to them and sat down.

"We're basing this on the colour of a house," Isabel said, watching Marilyn's movements. "It could be a coincidence."

"There are no coincidences around an anomaly," Dr Simon said.

Marilyn stared down at her handbag, a dull yellow satchel that her sister had given to her years ago, before the start of the Last War. An anomaly which extended to all points of the universe was an extraordinary thing; one could travel anywhere and anywhen. In the right hands, it could be a powerful defensive weapon; and in the wrong ones, a devastating offensive one. But whoever was in this anomaly was lost, truly lost. Even if they got inside, how could anyone be found in such a space? Or perhaps Miss Trudy's atoms had been distributed throughout the cosmos, each atom separated by eons of space and time; how could they ever bring her back together again?

"It had only vaguely occurred to me that this might be the case," Dr Simon said. "But I've been working on the assumption that the inside of an anomaly is discrete to a location or to a time. But if on its inside it is infinite… Well, this is magnificent."

"Not so hotso for Miss Trudy," Isabel said.

Marilyn took a sip of her tea and then carefully put the cup down. "You are missing one more thing, doctor."

"What's that?" he said. Isabel held her marker up in anticipation.

"Nothing happens around an anomaly by coincidence," Marilyn said.

"That's correct."

"Then, according to your own criteria, it is absolutely no coincidence that we received that letter."

"No, it may not be," said Dr Simon.

"And it was no coincidence that it was Miss Trudy who opened the letter," Marilyn said. "And not me."

"Oh, interesting," said Dr Simon.

"Oh my worlds," Isabel said. "You think that the letter wasn't just random good luck?"

"No," Marilyn said. "I think Miss Trudy was summoned."

* * *

BEFORE IT GOT DARK OUTSIDE, Dr Simon went out and shot and skinned a pair of rabbits for their dinner. They had agreed to bunk in at Warehouse 44 for the night and start the investigation again in the morning.

"We'll return to Mr Megal," Marilyn said. They were sitting at the back of the warehouse, an enormous old apple tree covering most of the sky in front of them, black against the dark blue of the twilight. They were munching on rabbit meat which the doctor had expertly cooked over a few Bunsen burners. "We need to find out more about Miss Trudy. Unless, Miss Isabel, you know anything about her?"

"Not me," Isabel said. "I never knew anything about this project. First I heard of you was when you walked into my office with that stone face of yours." She flashed a smile at Marilyn.

Dr Simon nodded. "The experiment would only work if nobody knew all the details. And the fewer people involved, the better."

"I wonder how many other projects he has that I don't know about," Isabel said, pensively. "I always thought I was in the know, you know?"

"How long have you worked for him?" Marilyn asked.

"Since the end of the Last War."

"But you must have been barely a teenager at the end of the Last War."

"No, I was almost 22," Isabel said, and there was a haughty note in her voice. Marilyn smiled in the darkness.

"So tell me about Miss Trudy," Isabel said.

"I'm afraid I don't have a lot to tell you." Marilyn shifted her position on the step and took off her hat, placing it carefully on the step next to her. "We weren't employees, you see. We were enthusiasts. We had a certain fiction we had to vigorously maintain. I know that she was very punctual. She has at least three or four good suits, and one or two poorer ones. She doesn't usually wear a hat. She has blonde hair which she always wore in a bob. And quite blue eyes, quite noticeable really. But the most important thing is…" Here Marilyn dropped her voice. "I always thought that she wasn't an enlistee."

Isabel glanced at Dr Simon. He was stretched out on the grass in front of them, staring up at the stars.

"Your age, is she?" said Isabel.

"Thereabouts. Perhaps a bit older."

"Not so interesting, is it?" said Isabel. "Most ladies don't enlist."

Marilyn gave Isabel one of her rare smiles. "I think Mr Megal employs a type, don't you?"

Isabel laughed. "Yes, I suppose so. All right. Tomorrow we start at Mr Megal's office. We need to find out who Miss Trudy was and why she was summoned."

"And then maybe we can figure out who summoned her," Dr Simon said dreamily.

"Do you have any theories, doctor?" Marilyn asked.

He rolled on to his side and looked at the two ladies.

"I thought you'd never ask!" he said. "My first supposition was that it had to be a person who either knew, or suspected strongly, that someone was running this project. To be honest, many of my colleagues are interested in this field, and may be running their own experiments. Although none with the backing of anyone so powerful as Mr Megal."

"Or rich," Isabel added.

"Indeed," the doctor said. "But to succeed, they would not only need to know the experiment was in progress; they would also need to know the location of the anomaly."

"But if they knew the location of the anomaly, why would they not investigate it themselves? Why would they send *you* a letter?" Isabel said.

"Exactly," said Dr Simon. "My next supposition was that it could just be someone who suspected there was an anomaly and wanted to test it out for themselves using the same methods that I had at first, sending out randomly addressed letters on a regular basis until they struck it lucky."

"But you said that didn't work, doc."

"Indeed. And in any case, I think we all agree that there are no chances or coincidences around an anomaly. Which means that the most unlikely thing of all is the most probable. Somebody who knew about the project, who also knew the location of the anomaly, AND knew that Miss Trudy was working on it."

Marilyn was silent for some moments as she considered this. "But that's literally impossible," she said finally. "Miss Trudy and I didn't know of any anomalies, nor did you or Mr Megal. And nobody outside of the project could have known the office existed or it would never have worked."

"Exactly," said Dr Simon. "Categorically, the project would not have worked, and Miss Trudy would not have disappeared, if anybody in the world had known of the existence of the Office of Dead Letters. It is a commendation to you, Miss Marilyn, and to Miss Trudy, that the experiment worked. Your vigorous adherence to the idea that it was a hobby and not a job, meant that it never became a stable place where the letter could have been delivered. So somebody knew of the office, knew of the anomaly, and yet the letter was still delivered."

"Physics isn't my bag, but I feel like a whole lot of laws are being messed with here," Isabel said. "But wait, doc, didn't *you* know of the existence of the office?"

"No. Even Mr Megal and I did not know of its whereabouts or what it was called. We merely knew that some enthusiasts had agreed to intercept mail that hadn't quite found its way to its destination."

"Miss Trudy named it," Marilyn said. "After we met you and got your brief. I found the office space and Miss Trudy named it. I thought she was being romantic, naming it after an impossible thing."

"So you see," said Dr Simon. "There's only one person who could have sent the letter."

"And who is that, doc?"

"Miss Trudy herself."

"Agh, doc, you keep contradicting yourself!" Isabel threw a rabbit bone off into the darkness. "She knew that her letter would be delivered to the office, so it couldn't have been Miss Trudy."

"Space time error," said the doctor. "Common mistake. She could have sent it at a time when she didn't know about the office. Right now, she is in all of time and space. If she could just find a way to exit the anomaly, she could go anywhere and anywhen and tell herself to send the letter."

"Doesn't sending herself a letter which starts the whole process create a paradox?" Isabel said. "The effect comes before the cause?"

"Yes, yes, but where Miss Trudy is, there is no before. Everything happens all at once."

"She's here, there, and everywhere?" said Isabel.

"Yes. And now, then and forever."

"Lucky Miss Trudy," said Isabel.

"I'm not so sure about that," said Marilyn, looking up at the stars. They were so very far away; she wondered what they felt like.

"This is a completely new state of being," said Dr Simon. "To exist in all places and all times, and yet confined to one place in our plane… We should give it a name." His mind raced through some options. "The Simon Principle? Simon's Law?"

"The Grayling Condition," said Marilyn.

"Ah yes," said the doctor. "Quite right." And he lay back on the ground to look up at the stars, at the sky, at the extent of the universe, and to think of all that could have been and all that would be.

8

The theoretical and the impossible

Isabel drove the Cab into the private garage under the Sky Tall Building.

"Hello, my beauties," she said in a whisper, looking at the four cars that were lined up on the left wall.

They took the elevator and descended into Megal's bunker. He was not surprised to see them.

Dr Simon laid out the situation while Megal made them coffee. Isabel moved several piles of comic books so that they could sit on the sofas, although Marilyn opted for the same hard-backed chair facing the lift doors she had chosen before.

"You want to find out about Miss Trudy?" said Mr Megal.

The investigative trio nodded.

"I don't have a great deal of information," Megal said. "But I dug out my notes in case they might be useful." He picked up a slender folder from a pile by his chair and handed it to Marilyn. She began to flip through it wordlessly while Megal watched her.

"What do you think?" he asked. He had put his coffee cup down and his hands were restless on his knees.

Marilyn looked up. "This is everything you have?"

Megal nodded.

She reached the last page and then her eyes opened wide. She pulled out the piece of paper to look at it more closely.

"What is it?" Isabel said.

"I don't say this very often," Marilyn said. "But I was wrong. Miss Trudy *had* enlisted."

"Of course she had," Megal said. "I can hide down here because I hire only the best up there." Megal pointed upwards, to the 11 floors above them. "But Miss Marilyn, you're surprised?"

Marilyn paused before answering. "Yes," she said, finally. "Miss Trudy had none of the hallmarks of an enlistee. Miss Isabel I picked out quite quickly, although she's awfully young."

Isabel snorted.

"But Miss Trudy ..."

Megal nodded. "Yes. Too scrawny, too sloppy, too cranky."

Isabel let out a low sound and Marilyn looked at Megal witheringly.

"No, Mr Megal. She didn't seem to have a developed ... sense of anything."

"Ah, yes," he said. "Of course. My apologies."

"But you don't have her records? Just this?"

Megal nodded.

Marilyn handed the folder to Isabel. "I'd be interested to know what you think."

"I'd be interested to know what other files I don't know about," Isabel said, taking the folder.

"So T1 and T2," Megal said. "Will they represent a complication?"

Dr Simon chimed in now. "I think they are elements of Miss Trudy. Somehow, with her entering the anomaly, some part of her has exited or morphed into the surrounding neighbours. Her presence inside the fold is affecting the normal fabric on either side."

"How big is the anomaly?" asked Megal.

"I believe it encompasses the entire universe in its interior," the doctor said, rather grandly.

"No, no," said Megal. "You keep talking about either side of the fold. But how far forward and backward does it extend? How high up? Could a bird fly into it? Does it go down into Underworld? Does it cross the street?"

Dr Simon opened his mouth then shut it again. "I …" He turned to face each of them in turn, but they just looked at him with expectant faces. "I hadn't considered that," he said.

Marilyn wondered, not for the first time, what exactly Dr Simon's specialty was.

"Oh," Isabel said. She was still reading through Trudy's file. "She was in the Philosophy Regiment."

"What does that mean?" Megal said.

"They deal with the theoretical and the impossible," Isabel said.

"That explains a great deal," said Marilyn.

"It does?" said Megal.

"But how do you know, Miss Isabel? There's no mention of her service. Only her discharge and medical records."

Isabel looked slightly embarrassed. "Well, she had a tonsillectomy at the hospital in Goodnight in the 2nd summer of the Last War. If she were a civilian, that wouldn't mean anything. But if she were a soldier, there were only two regiments there at that time, and she certainly wasn't in Heavy Arms."

"Certainly not," Marilyn said. "How do you know so much about troop displacement? Or do I not want to know?"

"I… I enjoy memorising trivial things."

"Like colours. And wartime movements," Marilyn said. "Well, Mr Megal, I'm not sure if you made a grave mistake or a stroke of genius when you hired Miss Trudy Grayling. Or indeed, perhaps you had less say in the matter than you think. Miss Trudy may have known far more about this project than would have made you comfortable. If she was in the Philosophy Regiment, it's quite possible that she knows more about space time rifts and anomalies than Dr Simon."

"I say," said the doctor, but then fell silent.

"So your theory that she sent herself the letter is not impossible?" said Megal.

"Nothing is impossible when you have all of space and time," the doctor said, and he sounded tired.

Marilyn sighed and stood up, slinging her satchel over her shoulder. "Well, theorising will only get us so far. I propose we visit Miss Trudy's home. And then I think we should return to Jellicoe Street and see if we can map out this anomaly or whatever else we can do to assist Dr Simon. We need to find if it has an entry point and if we can access it in our physical world. We don't know yet if Miss Trudy was involved, but we do know we have to attempt to find her and ask her if she needs to be rescued."

Megal stood too and beamed around at them. "I have to say, I invested in this project just because it sounded theoretically intriguing. But now it is proving to be …" He waved his hands around, looking for the right words.

"Challenging?" Marilyn offered.

"Consternating?" Isabel tried.

"Evidentially intriguing?" Dr Simon said.

"Better than a comic book," the billionaire finished.

9

Cardamom and spice

A fter they left Sky Tall Building, the trio made a detour so
that Marilyn could drop off the envelope in Encyc. She
had a contact, she said, who could do an in-depth analysis
of the envelope to see if it could provide them any clues.

"A chemist?" said Dr Simon, his professional curiosity piqued.

"Of a sort," Marilyn said. Isabel stopped the car in front of a
dusty cottage on a rundown street and Marilyn got out. "I won't be
long."

"Not the sort of place I'd expect someone like Miss Marilyn to
have contacts," Dr Simon said, scooting down in his seat and
peering over the edge of the window. "Are the doors locked, Miss
Isabel?"

"Doc, it's an open-topped car."

They looked over. Marilyn was talking with someone at the
partly-opened door. On either side of the house were a
leathermaker and a pawn shop, and the rest of the street was
populated by other low sorts of establishments.

"It's awfully close to Underworld here," Dr Simon said. "The
ground is thin. You can feel it."

Isabel turned to look at him.

"Didn't take you for a Bigger," she said, but without malice, just genuine interest.

"Oh, don't misunderstand me! I have the greatest respect for our Underworld cousins," Dr Simon said. Isabel noticed that he used the more distant 'cousins' rather than the more acceptable 'siblings.' "It's only their methods I disagree with. So unscientific. So wild."

They saw Marilyn turn to them and give a brief wave before she ducked into the low doorway.

"So you're enlistees," said Dr Simon. "I don't think I've ever met one before, let alone two."

Isabel snorted. "Don't keep company with women very often, Doc?"

He reddened a little. "Well, I don't exactly socialise out there in the Apple Quarter."

Isabel considered the man. He was in his late 30s, stereotypically unruly, and yet not unhandsome in a way.

"Do you stay out there always, then? Don't you have a home?"

"Oh, I did. But it's just easier, you know …" He trailed off and slumped back again into the seat.

"Yes," Isabel said. "I was an enlistee. Gosh, I don't say that out loud very often."

"Why is it such a blessed secret? Seems like something to be proud of."

Isabel was silent, wondering what exactly to say to the man. It's not that it was a blessed secret; but talking about it always raised questions, ones that most enlistees would rather not answer. And memories. So many memories that were better off left alone.

Isabel was startled by Marilyn opening the passenger side door. "Let's go," Marilyn said. "We'll need to come back later for her analysis."

"Yes ma'am," Isabel said. And she took off at speed, stirring up the dust of Encyc around them. They were off, back to Jellicoe Street and its odd inhabitants.

"Hm," Marilyn said, clutching her hat.

Isabel parked the car in front of the cosmic latte fence and they all looked across the road at number 13. Marilyn blamed herself for not thinking of the rest of the street on their last visit. Of course they should have investigated fore and aft of number 12, not just to its left and right, but they'd been so fixated on the two Tees. What a stupid rookie error. She took her hat off and fanned herself slightly. She didn't have Isabel's sense of smell; she was just hot.

"Well, it's certainly in the firing line," she said, and popped her hat back on. "Miss Isabel, shall we?"

The two women went over to number 13, leaving Dr Simon to wave his ineffectual wand against the fence some more. There didn't appear to be anyone at home, at least, nobody answered their knocks. Isabel did a quick circumnavigation to see if the back door were open, but the house seemed dreadfully quiet.

"All the same," Marilyn said. "It feels like someone is here. Although … Not someone, too."

"Another Tee?" Isabel said.

"Perhaps. What can you sense?"

Isabel took another sniff. "All I've got is you and me."

Short of breaking in, they had to leave it. The houses either side yielded perfectly ordinary suburban families who had noticed nothing unusual and who were evidently excluded from the effects of the anomaly.

They regrouped with Dr Simon who, unsurprisingly, had found nothing new.

"To Panko, then," said Marilyn, and Isabel nodded. Panko was where Trudy had lived, according to Megal's file.

"Even if she really knew nothing about this," Isabel said, starting up the car. "There might be someone waiting for her at home."

"I've never been to Panko!" Dr Simon said with delight. Once again, Marilyn wondered about his qualifications.

Panko was only a short distance as the crow flies, but having to detour around Rosie Mountain meant the drive was quite long. Isabel pulled into the busy ring road, crowded with cars and omnibuses and donkeys, and seemed unfazed by the traffic.

"I suppose she used to take the train, then," Marilyn said. She was feeling rather ill at ease, and it wasn't a feeling that came naturally to her. Now that fictions could be cast aside, she was able to think freely, and she realised that she had thought of Trudy as her friend, or at least a colleague – one about whom she'd evidently known nothing. Even things she had assumed or deduced had been utterly wrong. Marilyn had pictured Trudy as a spinster type, a graduate, one who had never enlisted because she thought she was too clever, too indispensable to civilian life. She imagined Trudy on a bicycle or walking to work each morning from Epic or somewhere just outside the City. It hadn't occurred to her that Trudy was a commuter from Panko, spending her mornings and evenings sitting side-by-side with journeymen, shop girls, and clerks. She hadn't known her at all.

Trudy's apartment was on the third floor of a plain building of the sort that Panko was famous for, if it were famous for anything. Isabel dealt with the lock, and she and Marilyn quickly scanned for an alarm or traps, but found none. It was a small apartment, just one bedroom, a kitchen and small living area, but it had a sensational view of Rosie Mountain and the Unnamed Lake.

Isabel looked around, took in the new furnishings, the modern kitchen.

"I didn't expect anything so swish in Panko," she said.

Marilyn pointed at the roll-top secretarial desk in the living room. "You take that. I'll take the bedroom."

"And me?" said Dr Simon.

"Kitchen," Marilyn said.

She went into Trudy's bedroom. There was no sign that anyone but the woman had lived here. The bed was made up neatly, a book on the left side table, and a stuffed toy fox on the bedspread. Marilyn opened the wardrobe. There were the several suits that she remembered well. There was also a gorgeous blue dress made of a very soft fabric. Marilyn took it gently in her hands. It was of the finest appleworm silk and was obviously very well made. Even with her gloves on, she could tell by the feel of it that the fabric was not from Overworld; it was not from any factory she knew of. She hesitated before taking off her gloves. It was such a personal item. But the more she knew of Trudy, the more likely she would be able to help her. She brushed her hand against the dress softly with the back of her knuckles, just trying to gently glean information rather than yank it out. The silk responded to her touch, drawing towards her. It was full of expectation, practically shivering with it. But the dress had never been worn; not by Trudy, not by anyone.

With a frown, Marilyn hung the dress back up inside the wardrobe. And there, at the end of the rack, amongst the heavy winter coats, was Trudy's uniform. Marilyn unhooked it and laid it out on the bed.

Overworld Defence Force uniforms were, as a rule, very plain. An experienced eye could discern certain peculiarities which would give away a person's position, but Marilyn couldn't see any of the stitches or pips that indicated rank. She ran her hands along the seams and over the buttons. She listened to the sounds the material made as it crinkled in her hands. She checked inside the pockets, but didn't feel anything. In short, Trudy's uniform was completely standard. It was as though the uniform had come straight from the dispensary. It had no history whatsoever – just like the dress.

Marilyn continued her way around the bedroom. The fox held no secrets, nor did any of Trudy's drawers. The usual array of undergarments and pyjamas, a few dirty magazines of the most general sort. It had been an unusually warm spring and Trudy's bed was already stripped of its winter bedclothes. There was only a thin sheet and a light lambswool blanket. Marilyn left the uniform on the bed and went out to the living area.

Isabel had clearly gone through everything thoroughly. The secretarial desk stood open with its few papers laid out in neat piles, the drawers standing out empty.

Isabel glanced up at her. "Nothing here, I'm afraid. Not even a photo. No commissions. No handwritten notes. Just bills and general knick knacks."

"I thought as much," said Marilyn. "I could use your help with something in the bedroom."

"Sure," Isabel said. She wiped her hands on her handkerchief and followed Marilyn.

"Ooooh," she whistled as she saw the uniform. She drew near

then leaned over and looked very carefully at the fabric as Marilyn had done. "Standard issue," she said. Then she closed her eyes and breathed in deeply.

"Well?" said Marilyn.

"You won't believe this," said Isabel. "General First Order."

"Are you sure? It feels normal to me."

"I'm sure. There's a hint of cardamom that's only found in the factory at Mini Atlas. And the only uniforms made there…" Isabel paused and then lowered her voice. "A General First Order, Miss Marilyn. That's way more than I expected."

"Yes," Marilyn said. "Miss Trudy's disappearance is turning out to be the least intriguing thing about her."

"Ladies!" Dr Simon called out. They went to join him in the large modern kitchen, its black and white walls spotless, the benches sleek and shiny.

"What have you found, doc?"

"Well, I certainly don't have the powers of deduction that you ladies possess, but I can almost guarantee that this kitchen has never been used for cooking."

"Yes, that seems evident," said Marilyn, after waiting for more.

Dr Simon was not deflated by this. "And is it also evident," he went on. "That the oven actually houses an extraordinary secret?"

Marilyn looked at the cast iron oven. Its chimney reached up into the ceiling as though it still used charcoal, but there was also a gas inlet – one of the very modern duo-ovens. It looked completely brand new, without a streak of grease or a smear of dust.

Dr Simon bent over and opened the cast iron door.

"Behold!" he said.

"Ah, doc," Isabel said, peering in. "It's empty."

"Are you certain, Miss Isabel?" said the doctor. And he pressed down on the two hobs. The whole top of the stove slowly raised up to the ceiling as if by hydraulics, and revealed a dark grey machine, plastic on the outside, a green glass screen facing them.

"Oh my Worlds," Isabel said. "How did she get a computer?"

"Hm," said Marilyn. "Hm!"

"I believe it's a Thinktank2000," said Dr Simon, stepping toward it with awe.

"Doctor!" Marilyn called out sharply. "Nobody move. Think about it. If you had an illegal computer in a fake oven in your unused kitchen, wouldn't you protect it?"

"Is the fake oven not protection enough?" the doctor said, but he had stopped in his tracks and remained still. They all scanned the walls and floor and ceiling carefully, rooted as they were to the spot, looking for any signs of a trap.

"There," Marilyn said, pointing to a black speck on the ceiling. It could have been anything: a fly, dirt. "Sensor bug."

Isabel nodded.

"Impossible!" said Dr Simon. "Those are forbidden in Overworld!"

"Nevertheless, Doctor, it persists."

"Can you hear anything?" Isabel said.

"Only that it is vibrating."

"It's probably already detected us then," said Isabel. "I don't have any actual experience with sensor bugs. Do you, Miss Marilyn?"

"None. We should leave immediately."

"Wait," said Dr Simon. "We can't just leave the Thinktank here."

"The bug will take wing at any moment," said Marilyn. "We have no idea what its orders will be. We must leave." She didn't move, though. Who knew what the bug was waiting for before flying off to cause whatever mayhem Miss Trudy had laid in store for intruders?

"Can't we just kill it?" said Dr Simon. "I'm an excellent shot. Just give me a stone. Or the pepper mill there."

"Doctor," said Isabel. "It's a sensor bug, not a rabbit. Its shell was forged in the Underground River of Lava. It is not going to be harmed by a *pepper mill*."

"Think," Marilyn said. "What traps could be laid for us in a domestic apartment?"

"A sensor bug has a limited range of motion," the doctor said.

"It can only fly a few metres. So it's something within the kitchen itself."

"The gas!" said Isabel. "That would make a capital bomb. I'm with Miss Marilyn. We should leave before it –"

With a buzz that only Marilyn could hear, the black speck flew from its spot, too fast and tiny to follow where it went.

"Dammit," said Isabel, as all the lights suddenly went out, plunging them into darkness. They heard the kitchen door slam shut behind them. Marilyn hurled her body against it but it was firm and didn't budge.

They started to cough as they were overwhelmed with a stifling smell of chilli and spices.

"Quick doctor," said Marilyn. "Is it the gas? You're the explosives expert. What should we do?"

"I literally have no idea," said the doctor. "Is this how it ends then? In Panko? In a *kitchen*?"

"What can you smell, Miss Isabel? Is it gas?"

"No, I can't smell anything but kitchen spices," Isabel said, her voice higher than usual. "She's smart. Miss Trudy is damn smart."

"Doctor, cover your face," Marilyn said. She could hear him fumbling about in the dark.

"Uhve already done that," came the doctor's muffled voice.

Marilyn had taken off her own blazer and wrapped it around her nose and mouth. She strained to listen for the sensor bug, to figure out where it had gone to set off the cavalcade of spices, the door, the lights. Finally her hand found the gas inlet, but she could feel that it was empty; there was no gas flowing through it to suffocate them. What on earth was the trap then?

"Chlorine!" Isabel yelled. "I can smell it now! It's chlorine. Quickly, remove your clothing and throw it to me."

Marilyn stripped off her heavy outer skirt and blouse and threw them towards Isabel's voice. She could hear Dr Simon fumbling with his own clothes, and the enlistee tearing things off shelves until with a grunt she found what she was looking for. Marilyn became aware that she could now just make out the shape of Dr Simon next to her; there was a faint light coming from the computer.

A single line of text was displayed on its frontispiece.

"Pass the word," it said.

"What word?" said the doctor.

"It's contained," Isabel yelled out. "Chlorine ball activated by a simple drop mechanism attached to the door. I've wrapped it up tight, but it's still mildly toxic in here. The sooner we get out the better."

They all faced the computer and its line of text. Below the glass there was an input device attached by a cable. Marilyn reached her hands out to it and hovered them above the keys.

"It's buzzing," she said. She started to explore the keys with her fingertips, closing her eyes, both listening and feeling.

"You've touched one before?" said the doctor.

"Shh…" said Isabel. "Let her work."

Eventually, Marilyn put both her hands completely onto the input device, pressed some of the keys, and then they were all suddenly bathed in a white electric light from an overhead panel.

"Welcome, Trudy Whiting," came a voice from the computer.

"Whiting?" said Isabel.

"It can speak?" said Dr Simon.

The kitchen door quietly swung open, letting in fresh air. Isabel grabbed the clothing-wrapped chlorine ball and confined it in the bathroom, while the doctor thrust a frypan in the kitchen door jamb so it couldn't unexpectedly close on them again.

"I say," he said, standing upright and remembering he was only in his underwear. He glanced over at Marilyn who was standing at the computer terminal in a petticoat, her long legs exposed. He turned away, but ran straight into Isabel who was returning wearing nothing but a shift and bloomers. "I say…" he said again.

Isabel smiled and gave him a pat on his bare ginger arm. "You could do with a bit more daylight, doc. I never saw skin so white." She jumped and sat up on the kitchen bench, nothing but white skin and legs herself. "All right, Miss Marilyn, spill. What's on the Thinktank?"

The glass screen was now full of numbers and letters and Marilyn tapped the key panel cautiously, moving through them.

"I believe it's an algorithm," she said.

"Makes sense," said Isabel. "The Thinktank2000 was designed to crack codes during the Last War But One. I thought Underworld had torched them all after they won."

"There were always rumours that some had been salvaged," Marilyn said. "Doctor, do you have any ideas?"

The doctor, his arms folded across his bare chest, leaned forward to stare at the frontispiece. He shook his head slowly.

"I'm not sure. It could almost be the same equations I've been working on, trying to find anomalies in time and space. May I?" He took over the arrow keys from Marilyn and used them to move around the equation. "But it seems to start with a completely different premise. I'd need to really spend some time with it to know for sure."

"Excellent," Marilyn said. "We've done all we can here. Miss Isabel, please arrange to have this computer extracted and brought to Mr Megal's office. Unless, doctor, you'd prefer it in the Apple Quarter?"

"Mr Megal's office is fine," the doctor said.

Marilyn's skirt was still salvageable from the chlorine ball, but she grabbed a cardigan from Trudy's wardrobe, the blouses all being too small. Isabel took a suit for herself, while the doctor donned a pair of Trudy's pyjamas, the wormsilk falling in elegant cascades down his long limbs.

"I could get used to this," he said, twirling in the lounge room.

"And wormsilk is naturally fire-retardant," Isabel said with a smile.

"Indeed?" the doctor said.

Trudy's uniform was still lying on the bed where Marilyn had left it and after Trudy and Dr Simon had finished dressing, she took the uniform and hung it back in the wardrobe. Once again, she touched the beautiful blue dress and wondered what event it had been bought for. She regretted that she could only feel the history of an object, not its intent or its future. As she closed the cupboard door, Marilyn caught sight of the book on the bedside table. She picked it up and felt the smooth leather tingle against her fingertips with a curious unknown energy. There was no dust jacket and the title was not embossed on the cover. Marilyn opened the book and saw the title printed on the first page.

A Letter to Merry Lynn, it was called. By Tee Rudy Grayling.

* * *

BACK AT JELLICOE STREET, a wind stirred the leaves, causing them to eddy in front of number 13. A woman out walking her dog passed by, pulling her collar up and tightening her jacket against the breeze, in spite of the mildness of the day. There was something biting about the wind, as if it could cut through anything – a jacket, a wool scarf, a person's skin.

Or even space time itself.

At number 13, behind the curtain, someone watched and waited.

10

Senses and sensibilities

Marilyn, Isabel and Simon gathered in Mr Megal's den, the four of them feasting on fried rice from Sino Town. Dr Simon was using Sino-sticks, but the rest chose to use their fingers.

"It's mind-bogglingly similar to some of the stuff I was working on," the doctor said, holding his sticks in the air. "I mean, if I didn't know better, I'd almost say it *was* my work."

"How do you know it's not?" said Megal. He leaned over to dip a roll into the hot sauce, but glanced up at the doctor. "It might be yours. Miss Trudy knew of you and your work and could have… acquired your data."

"No, definitely not." The doctor paused. "Because, well, frankly, because it's right and mine is not. I can understand the working out, but what is different is where Miss Trudy has begun. She starts with a set of assumptions that are as yet opaque to me."

They all glanced over at the computer. Isabel had arranged a trusted gang of outfitters to pull it from Trudy's apartment and smuggle it into the den, where it now sat at the edge of the cavern.

"I don't understand how you unlocked it," Megal said.

"It's hard to explain," said Marilyn. She was still wearing Trudy's black cardigan over her petticoat, but the chlorine smell of her skirt had proved too much and she now sat with a blanket covering her legs. For a moment, Megal imagined her as an old lady, reading a book by the fire, or out in the garden, curls of hair coming loose from her bun, her hands covered in dirt, throwing him a rare smile over her shoulder. "I could feel it," she was saying, and he came back to attention. "I could feel what Miss Trudy would type when she was in there."

"Did her password give you any clues?" Isabel asked.

Marilyn shook her head. "Seems like a random selection of letters and numbers. But I'll write it down for you if you'd like to exercise your cryptographic brain."

"That'd be neat," Isabel said. "I mean, I'm just glad you got us out of there."

"Yes, I really don't want to die in Panko," Dr Simon said. "The shame of it! Not that the Apple Quarter is much better."

"You don't like your laboratory, doctor?" said Megal, with a hint of steel.

"Oh! No! That's not what I mean. I love my lab. Very excellent. Most wonderful," said Dr Simon, backtracking beautifully. He was still wearing Miss Trudy's pyjamas having declined the offer of a pair of Megal's trousers.

"It was not a pleasant place to be trapped, that's for sure," said Isabel. "That kitchen."

Mr Megal had finished eating and he leaned back in his bean-bag chair.

"So. So far, we have found that Miss Trudy Grayling, also known as Miss Trudy Whiting, was not only aware of the dead letter experiment, but was also investigating it herself. We presume that she was trying to find an anomaly using her own means. So do we think she sent the letter to herself?"

"I have left the envelope with a contact," Marilyn said. "When we pick it up tomorrow morning, I believe we will know exactly who sent the envelope and from where. Possibly even when."

"Excellent work," said Megal.

"There's something else. Miss Trudy left me an encrypted message. I hesitate to share it with you because I'm afraid it may be classified information."

Isabel leaned forward. "Are you still active?"

"No, not since Year 1."

"Me neither. But you think Miss Trudy still is?" Marilyn nodded. Isabel let out a long heavy sigh. "I'd heard some people still were, but…"

"I'm sorry," said Dr Simon. "I have no idea what you're talking about. Why are you enlistees always so damn cryptic? What's the big secret?"

Marilyn and Isabel exchanged a look and then Isabel began.

"There's no secret, doc," Isabel began. "We were specially trained operatives during the Last War."

"Well, I already know that much at least," said the doctor.

"And as you also no doubt know, we are all women. The crucial thing is that we enlisted. We were never recruited or drafted. We are individual operatives. Being an enlistee gives you certain privileges, access to certain… opportunities that you might not otherwise have if you were part of the general forces."

"Heightened senses," Dr Simon said.

"Yes, exactly. As you probably noticed, I can smell things that others can't. And Miss Marilyn appears to have heightened touch."

"And hearing," Marilyn added.

"A two-hander," Isabel said with a rueful smile.

"But why must you be enlistees?" said Dr Simon.

Here, Megal cut in with some impatience. "Doctor, if they are recruits, they can't be modified for war under the Articles of the Two Worlds. You know, 'no recruited soldier, nor any man who fights for Overworld, may use Overworld knowledge in wars between the Two Worlds', etc, etc," he said.

Realisation dawned on the doctor's face.

"You're using Overworld knowledge in the wars against Underworld?" he said. "It's a sneaky get around!"

Isabel laughed. "Well, I haven't heard it called that before. But yes, basically we can modify ourselves because we're not recruits and we're not men. We're enlistees and can do what we like."

"Like pirates," Simon said.

"We are not pirates!"

"Perhaps privateers," Marilyn said, with a smile.

"Then Miss Trudy could be fighting for anyone," said Dr Simon. She could be a 'privateer' for Underworld for all we know."

Marilyn shook her head. "The Last War is over. The geography is settled for the first time in hundreds of years. Overworld won definitively."

"So if Miss Trudy is still active, who is she fighting against?" Isabel asked.

"A new enemy perhaps," said Marilyn. "Or a very old one."

They passed the night in Megal's den, which Isabel furnished with several cots from the maintenance department. As she listened to the sounds of everyone settling down, shifting, coughing, she smiled.

"It's just like being back on duty," she said quietly. It was unclear who she was talking to.

"You must have been a baby when you enlisted," Marilyn said.

Isabel was silent a moment.

"Not a baby," she said. "But too young."

The quietness of the room was broken only by the gentle snoring of the doctor, who clearly could sleep anywhere. Megal was on his favourite sofa, as he often was, but not usually with three other people sharing his space. He stared at the ceiling, thinking of the missing woman. Most of his female employees were enlistees, and he had a fair number of male recruits, as well. He actively sought out the enlistees, knowing that they were astonishing people. It wasn't always easy to find them. Little things – their propensity for Bentley's shoes, enigmatic smiles, the way they seemed to be looking all around and through you as well as at you. Odd moments in their employment histories where they claimed to work in grocery stores or other implausible places. As he had said, he kept himself safe by surrounding himself with trustworthy people, the best. So how had Trudy Grayling evaded him?

He didn't have developed senses himself, but he knew when someone was lying to him. He knew people; but he had not known Miss Trudy Grayling aka Whiting.

Megal had come from privilege and had inherited a formidable and powerful name. But it was he who had built the business to the massive juggernaut it now was through careful and crucial investments during the Last War. Naturally, he had deplored the conflict. But the complete separation of Overworld from Underworld was the only way to achieve lasting peace, to finally end the decades of wars that had plagued generations. So he wasn't one to baulk at the opportunities the war had presented. His trade had not been weapons like the Barons, but property. He had acquired ruined building after ruined building, one of the first to understand that as the land settled the geography would change. Places that had been far away were now the heart of the City – and he owned most of it.

So as he lay there on his sofa, Megal was annoyed to the point of anger. How could Miss Trudy, who he had taken for some minor character, an enlistee but insignificant, how could she have deceived him so thoroughly?

More disturbingly, she had deceived Miss Marilyn, too. He trusted Miss Marilyn completely, even more than he trusted Miss Isabel, who was always the most competent person in a five-kilometre radius. He wondered if he'd made the right decision, putting Miss Marilyn in the dead letter experiment instead of his own office. Surely he could have found a role for her at Megal Enterprises, somewhere she could have been close…

He remembered her touch, the feel of her skin when they'd shaken hands at her interview. It had been electric and he had never been able to forget it. Had it simply been her special sense? What had she learned about him in that moment?

And now there she was, not a metre away in her cot, so close he could almost hear her breathing. And she, he thought, with a tremendous hot flush that shot all the way through him, she could hear him, his breathing, his heartbeat, every movement he made…

No. Definitely. He had done the right thing. Miss Marilyn had been more valuable in the dead letter experiment. He had definitely made the right decision sending her there. Unquestionably. He rolled over on his sofa and tried and tried to go to sleep.

11

Memories and order

In the morning, Dr Simon sat groggily at the Thinktank, sipping a coffee and making grunting noises. They had agreed that as well as working on the algorithm, he should search the computer to find any clues of who Trudy was working with.

"Not who she was working for?" Simon had asked.

Marilyn gave him a solid side eye.

"No, not *for*," she said. "With."

"And what can I do?" Megal said, as they finished up their simple breakfast.

"I have an idea," Simon said, turning to them. He had pastry crumbs down the front of the pyjama shirt, but didn't seem to notice. "There's a chap I know... Used to know. He helped me with my initial calculations. He may be able to help with Miss Trudy's algorithm."

"Of course," Megal said. "Just give Miss Isabel his details and she'll have him summoned. You can use one of our offices upstairs."

"I'm afraid that won't do," said Dr Simon. "We move in rather different circles these days and he can't really be fetched – not even to Sky Tall Building."

"Can't be fetched?" Megal said with a frown. He had a suspicion where this was going.

"But you could go to him, Mr Megal. He's a member of The Club."

"I'll make sure your suit is ready," Isabel said with alacrity.

"Not so fast," Megal said, turning on his secretary.

"What? You can't go to the Club dressed like that!" Isabel gestured at her employer's crumpled clothing, his mismatched socks.

"Well, no, obviously not like this," he said. "But the Club? I haven't been in years. I may not even be a member anymore."

"All the Megals are lifelong members, as you know perfectly well," said Isabel. "And you were there six weeks ago for the swearing in of your nephew so don't make up any further nonsense." She reached behind the sofa cushions for the receiver, plugged it into a socket by the desk and began talking to someone on the other end.

"This fellow better be worth it," Megal said.

"Oh, he is," said Dr Simon. "He's a genius. But he has… family issues."

"Your suit will be ready for you on Floor 11 with Miss Amanda," Isabel said. "If you'll kindly proceed."

Megal stepped into the elevator, grumbling, while the ladies prepared to head back to Jellicoe Street.

"Third time lucky!" Isabel said, but Marilyn did not feel quite as cheery. Third time lucky simply meant that they had failed twice already.

"Look, Marilyn, I know you're worried. But Miss Trudy…" Isabel dropped her voice. "She was a general. First Order, remember? You don't get there on good looks or luck."

In spite of herself, Marilyn smiled. It was the unofficial motto of the enlistees – not looks nor luck, just hard truck.

"So third time *successful*, then," said Marilyn.

"That's the spirit," said Isabel with a wink. She threw a goodbye over her shoulder to Dr Simon, who hunched over the computer and barely noticed them leave.

The ladies waited in the lobby for Megal, and Marilyn had a

chance to observe the people who worked and visited Megal Enterprises. A smart lot – she could almost feel the education on them. Graduates, all of them, but she could detect the occasional enlistee. This is what she had fought for, why she had enlisted as soon as she could – for science and technology and education for all. For a brighter future. Not for her own benefit, but for everyone in Overworld. For these people. But they were so foreign to her, these clever youngsters. She wondered what they were making, what they were creating, inventing, changing. What – she paused in her thoughts as two men, dressed in the finest brocade, walked past – colossal amounts of money they were spending.

The elevator dinged once again and Marilyn looked to see what bright young engineer would be disgorged this time. The doors opened to reveal an elegantly dressed man of commanding height and a face that spoke power.

"Mr Megal!" she said.

He was in an exquisite suit of charcoal grey, a red silk tie neatly tied around his neck, and in one hand he held a gold-tipped cane. Gone was the scruffy comic-book-reading man she had met before. She could finally see something of the businessman he was famed to be.

"You've gone the whole hog," said Isabel, raising her eyebrows at the cane.

Megal glanced down at the offending article and opened his mouth, ready to protest.

"You look outstanding," Marilyn said. He looked her directly in the eyes and she saw how pleased he was. And quite unbidden, she could hear the beat of his heart, heard it hasten as he gazed upon her.

"Shall we go?" she said, turning to Isabel.

"Let's hop to it," Isabel said. "We'll drop you at The Club on our way, boss."

The Club was only a few blocks away on Exxo Street, and Isabel drew the Cab up right in front.

"Ladies," said Megal, after he exited, giving them a brief salute with his cane. The ladies dipped their heads and then

Isabel took off with a roar, pinning them both to the back of their seats.

"Haha!" she said. "I hope those toffs at the Club heard that!"

She had an irrepressible energy and even Marilyn felt a little elated. Somehow they both knew – they were close to something. They had all the pieces in front of them. The office, the letter, Trudy's disappearance, the anomaly at Jellicoe Street and the strange people who lived there, and finally the revelation that Trudy may have known much more than any of them. It felt like they should be able to just reach out and rearrange the pieces until everything snapped into place, like an Underworld charm puzzle.

Their way out of the City was relatively free of traffic. Isabel put the radio on and they each sat in their own thoughts, watching the new buildings flick by, humming to the latest tunes.

"Do you remember what this was like, before the war?" Isabel asked.

"Yes," said Marilyn. "Do you?"

"Not really. I was mostly in the north." Isabel paused and Marilyn recognised the default desire to not reveal too much personal information. "That's where I'm from, originally. The north."

Marilyn knew how badly the north had fared during the Last War, and the Last War But One, but she chose not to say any trite condolences. It made sense now why Isabel had enlisted so young; she had probably lost a lot, if not everything.

"This was Underworld land," Marilyn said. "Lush and green, beautiful hills, sheep, lots of sheep. My word, Miss Isabel, you never saw so many sheep. You have cows in the north, yes?"

Isabel nodded. "Can't walk five metres without bumping into one."

"My sister and I would come out here to take picnics."

"Weren't you afraid of the Underworlders?"

"They left us alone," Marilyn said. "We were just there to enjoy the land, and they respected that. They're not bad people."

"Oh, I know that," Isabel said. Marilyn glanced over at her. If Isabel had seen half of what Marilyn had, then she had had her fair

64

share of trauma during the Last War. Nobody and nothing was unchanged by it. She wondered what pre-war Isabel had been like. Not that she really knew what Isabel was like now, she thought. She had been so mistaken about Trudy.

"When the war started, this land went into flux," Marilyn said. "The hills disappeared, and the sheep. I fought several battles here."

"That must have been hard," Isabel said.

"Yes."

"So you were fifth division, then?" Isabel said.

"Yes. How did you know?"

"Only 3rd and 5th divisions fought on the City limits. And there weren't any enlistees in 3rd division, only recruits."

"You have a prodigious memory," Marilyn said.

Isabel shrugged. "I memorise everything I read."

"I've never heard of that particular upgrade. Is that part of your enlistee enhancements?"

"No, I've always had that. It's like my party trick. I can remember anything. I can help others to remember, too." Isabel glanced over at Marilyn. "Like, I've been thinking, you're having the envelope checked, but what about the letter itself?"

"I assumed it was with Miss Trudy."

"But she read it? You said she opened the letter and read it?"

"Yes, I believe so."

"And?" said Isabel. "Did she say something? Do something? Make a noise?" Isabel turned down the radio.

Marilyn tried to think of that morning exactly as it had happened. She remembered being at her desk, her basket of interrupted letters, Trudy opposite her, the ticking of the clock, the slant of the sun coming through the window.

"She stood up," Marilyn said. "She opened the envelope with her knife, took the letter out and unfolded it. She stood up and made a noise like 'oh'. And then she disappeared."

Marilyn could hardly believe it had only happened the morning before yesterday. It felt much further away in time.

"But you know what that means?" said Isabel. "There was a clue in the letter. She knew she'd found it!"

"Well, yes, of course," said Marilyn.

"So what would a letter like that say? *Hey ladies. Hey Miss Trudy. Hey Office of Dead Letters?* It can't just have been a normal letter."

Marilyn was thoughtful. "Maybe it was a normal letter, but she felt something. We don't know what her sense is."

"Tell me again what happened," Isabel said and Marilyn repeated what she'd already said.

"Let's try this properly," Isabel said and, glancing over her shoulder, she pulled the Cab off the main road and into a quiet subdivision where new houses were going up faster than Aldovan mushrooms. Marilyn glanced at the pre-fab townhouses, and wondered what had happened to all those sheep.

"Well, Miss Isabel," Marilyn said. "What have you got for me?"

"Was she looking at the letter when she stood up?" Isabel said. "When she said 'oh'? Close your eyes. Breathe carefully. Now think only about Miss Trudy. Remove everything else from your mind and focus only on Miss Trudy."

Marilyn did as she was told. She cleared her mind and pictured Trudy standing at her desk, her blonde bob framing her white face, holding the letter. Her mouth was open and her eyes were wide, but where was she looking?

"Now look at the letter in her hand. Can you see it? Can you describe it?"

Marilyn let her mind drift deeper into the memory. She focused on the letter in Trudy's hand, the size and shape of the paper. It was small, like a page torn from a notebook. Trudy was clutching the bottom of it so tightly that it was almost crumpled in her hand.

"I see it," Marilyn said.

"Good. Now think only about where Trudy was looking when she stood up. Picture only her eyes," said Isabel. "Focus only on Miss Trudy's eyes."

Marilyn's internal gaze ran up the length of Trudy's arm, up her neck, to her plain face. Her eyes, that startling blue that she had somehow lent to T1 and T2, were wide. Marilyn had never known Trudy to be anything but calm and the look in her eyes – was it fear? Was it delight? – was enough to make even Marilyn shocked.

"Where is she looking, Miss Marilyn?" Isabel's voice came through to her. "Where is Miss Trudy looking?"

"Yes," Marilyn said, after a long period of silence. "I can see it. Her eyes are on the paper, moving back and forth. She was reading it before she disappeared."

Isabel guided Marilyn back out of her memory and then gave her a huge grin. "You did it! She read it! She read something in the letter that let her know she'd found it. I knew it. A General First Order doesn't give herself away that easily, you know. She was genuinely smashingly surprised."

"Yes, I believe you're right," said Marilyn.

"It can't have been an ordinary letter, then," said Isabel. "The doctor was right about one thing: there is absolutely nothing accidental about this whole thing. Miss Trudy was there all along for a reason. But if she was really surprised, maybe even *she* didn't know what that reason was."

Isabel restarted the Cab and drove back towards Jellicoe Street, babbling away excitedly and unable to stop smiling. But Marilyn wondered if she herself had also been in the office all along for a reason that she didn't yet know about. Or was she the one accident in this whole situation?

There was still the book she had found in Trudy's apartment, which she hadn't explicitly told the others about. She'd had only a few moments to look at it. It seemed to be a perfectly normal novel, a sprawling romance from one of the wars. It was obviously a message to her from Trudy, maybe too obviously. Clearly, the book was in code; but it would take a long time to decipher and she had more direct leads to pursue right now.

She hadn't been this stimulated for a long time. Not since she'd been on active duty during the war. That was more than two years ago now, and life had been peaceful since then, even with all the changes to Overworld. She had spent those two years opening letters in a small office and now she was back on the road, back in action, and she was feeling a little weary.

"Right, Miss M," Isabel said, interrupting her reverie. "Let's find this anomaly once and for all."

"What exactly are we going to do?" said Marilyn.

Isabel stared at her. "I thought you had a plan? Isn't that what you've been thinking about all this time you've been quiet?"

"No, I... I've been thinking how unprepared I am for all this now. How did we do it before?"

"Well, we had orders. We carried them out."

"You know what I mean," said Marilyn. "The stuff we didn't have orders for. The things we did on our own. How did we know?"

"You know, I never met an enlistee who wasn't as smart as an apple worm," said Isabel. "People forget what it takes to enlist. The sorts of women who *can* enlist. You'll never find a graduate or a baroness enlisting. Not because they're scared, but because they can't see what we see."

"And what's that?"

"The big picture," said Isabel. "What it really means for Overworld to be separate and how that makes lives better for both the Two Worlds. But more important than that, we can also see all the tiny parts that make up the big picture, in a way that politicians and barons and even generals often can't. That's why I admire Mr Megal; he's got an enlistee's mentality."

Marilyn thought again of an Underworld charm puzzle; how when the pieces came together, the whole magically became bigger than the sum of its parts. Of course, Underworlders didn't call it magic; they said it was their Knowledge. But they refused to share that Knowledge and so to the Overworlders it looked like magic. She had always supposed that Overworld Knowledge must often look like magic to them, too.

"What if there isn't one anomaly?" Marilyn said.

"I'm listening."

"We've assumed T1 and T2 are affected by the anomaly that has swallowed up number 12. But what if they are actually pieces of the anomaly? Did you ever see an Underworld charm puzzle?"

Isabel thought a moment. "You think if we bring them together, they'll... Recreate Miss Trudy?"

"I don't know. But it feels like the right thing to do."

"It feels like a hard thing to do!" said Isabel. "But I'm with you."

Marilyn outlined her plan. Isabel was to do all she could to convince the two Tees to come stand together at the fence.

"Right on top of the fucking anomaly?" Isabel said with a smile. "And you?"

"I'm going to get the last piece of the puzzle," Marilyn said and she walked across the street.

* * *

As MARILYN APPROACHED 13 Jellicoe Street, she had the sense again of someone watching. The walls were not cosmic latte, but it had definitely been touched by the anomaly. Now that she'd been to Jellicoe Street so many times, she thought she could perhaps feel it, where its edges were and where it began – and it began here.

She shook her head. She should have dealt with 13 more firmly before. Well, this time she wasn't taking 'no' for an answer. Indeed, she wasn't going to ask questions.

She walked directly to the window and rapped on it sharply.

"Hello!" she said. "I know you're there. I will talk to you."

All of this was pure instinct, she knew that. Bringing the two affected women together could be disastrous; she had no idea what the consequences would be. But all along they had been missing a vital piece of the puzzle and her gut told her it was here, at number 13.

"Come out," Marilyn said. There was no response. She let herself listen in and she could hear the unmistakeable heartbeat of a human. There was also a kind of echoing heartbeat, something she had never heard before, possibly a result of the anomaly.

"That's an order."

Then finally, she heard someone approach the door and it opened slightly.

"What do you want?" came a voice. It was very deep and hollow and Marilyn had the sense that it was coming from much further inside the house.

"Come out where I can see you," Marilyn said.

There was no movement behind the door, just a waft of stale air, and another smell that Marilyn couldn't place but which was familiar.

"Soldier, you're being called up," Marilyn said, and she pushed against the door which gave easily. In the front hall stood a woman, deeply hunched over so that her face was almost as low as her knees. She was rocking back and forth and side to side.

"Don't hurt an old woman," the voice said, but it was completely flat, without fear or emotion.

"You're no old woman," Marilyn said. Because inside the house she now knew she was right. She could hear it clearly in the woman's voice.

It was Trudy's voice.

"General," said Marilyn. The woman stopped rocking. "Tell me where you are."

"I am here," said the woman. "I am there. I am everywhere."

She seemed to be moving with great strain and Marilyn realised she was trying to look up. Whatever was wrong with her back was not feigned, then. The woman slowly, laboriously lifted her neck and turned her face up to Marilyn's.

The face had a forehead, a nose, a mouth. But where the eyes should be there was just smooth skin.

"They took them. They took my eyes," the woman said, and she laughed and laughed.

12

The Club and the computer

Megal felt the weight of history as he entered The Club. It was a solid bastion of Overworld, unaffected by wars and shifting geography. He resisted the urge to fix his tie, to fiddle, to be anything but cool and suavely sophisticated – an unwritten requirement of being a member of a club so exclusive that it was known simply as The Club.

"I can do this," he thought to himself. "I have done this countless times." And he promised himself a long quiet night in his den with the latest edition of Stargirl.

"Mr Megal, what a delight," said the Undersecretary in a tone which may or may not have been delighted. He took Megal's cane and placed it behind him in a wooden alcove which bore a bronze plague emblazoned with the Megal name. Megal thought briefly of the long line of Megals before him who had had their own canes – and hats and coats and cases – placed in this very spot. It was such an odd concept, all that history, back before The Last War had started when the Two Worlds were united. Back to the Last War But One, when Overworld had first tried for separation. All the way back past the Previous War and the More Previous War, back to the War of Our Grandparents – even then, the Megal name had been known. So much history, so much bloodshed, and always there had been The Club and a Megal in it.

"Is it?" Megal replied to the Undersecretary, in a tone that indicated he didn't care one way or the other. "I want to talk to a chap. Name of Barwell." Honorifics weren't required in The Club as they were all gentlemen.

"You will find von Barnwell in the smoking lounge," said the Undersecretary, closing his eyes and giving a nod towards the double doors that led into the sacred interior.

Megal rapped the counter with his knuckles as a thank you, and carried on inside. The first room was the sprawling library where he immediately felt several pairs of eyes casually scrutinising him over folded newspapers.

He had no time for these Club types who hung about all day. They spent their mornings reading tat and gossip, and their evenings in the gaming parlour, and a cursed lot of hours in between pretending to pass the time but really just wasting it. He thought of his own comic collection at Sky Tall, but that was different. He had worked hard during the war; he still worked hard now, but he also made time for leisure, to rest his busy brain. These men were merely winners of the spoils of war, but none of them had fought a day in their lives or worked for their money and standing. The Megals had always been enterprising and never shirked work – or duty to Overworld.

He perused the newspaper table in the centre of the room but it was the usual ragtag of political nonsense that turned his stomach. Not a decent human being among the political classes, and yet they were all still trying to take credit for winning the war. Ha! It had been businessmen like him who had won the war, and enlistees like Miss Trudy, Miss Marilyn and Miss Isabel, fearless warriors who had had their contributions quietly erased so that what they had done would never be known. Not to mention all the countless regular recruits who had died in their thousands, mere fodder in the battle to attain the separation of Overworld. The politicians had next to nothing to do with it.

"Mr Megal," came a very low voice at his side.

He turned to see a youngish man, one that he didn't recognise. Newspapers around the room rustled at this clear breach of etiquette; the silence of the library was sacrosanct.

"I must speak to you," the man said, his voice not quite low enough to avoid a quiet chorus of *ahems* and *harumphs*.

Megal nodded and the two walked through to the dining room. Megal's college chum Malagrassi was there, eating a whole chicken, and Megal gave him a brief wave. In a corner sat Burton and Collins, deep in conversation and sharing a bottle of claret.

"What will you have?" Megal said superciliously, choosing a table and sitting in one of the deep leather chairs.

It was amazing how easily this all came to him, the fiction of the Club, the playacting of it all.

"Oh, it's no mind to me," said the young man, and Megal ordered the claret, taking his lead from the other men. He could hardly remember the menu and it seemed easiest, although he was a terrible daytime drinker. Always made him cranky afterwards.

"Not a connoisseur of the finer side of life?" Megal said.

"Not interested," said the young man shortly. "It's just fuel. Everything here is just fuel." He waved his hand to indicate the Club.

"Well," said Megal when the waiter had brought their wine. "And who might you be and what do you want?"

"I know about Dr Simon's experiment," said the young man. "My name is von Barwell. I helped him with his early equations."

"Well, that was easy," said Megal. "You're just the chap I was looking for." And he raised his glass with a smile.

* * *

BACK AT SKY TALL BUILDING, Dr Simon was tapping his pen against his teeth as he read through line after line of data on the Thinktank. Occasionally, he would shout out aha! And write down a few notes. But mostly he was just feeling his spirits sink lower and lower with every minute that passed.

Miss Trudy must have been a genius. He could come up with no other word than that. Her complicated algorithm was a work of breathtaking beauty. He was able to follow the mathematics from a certain point and it all made sense, but the beginning refused to resolve for him. He could not understand what Miss Trudy's starting assumptions were and without them he was lost. He could pick up the thread eventually, but without understanding the start of the algorithm, he lost sight of the whole.

His own start had been so promising. Back before they'd established the Office of Dead Letters, he had made significant progress with his calculations, enough for Megal to believe in and fund him. They had met at a game night; they were both keen amateur Ambular players. They had been cast on the same team several games in a row and Megal had teased Simon for being covered in ink and burns.

"You laugh now, but when I bend space and time to my will, you'll be interested then," Simon had retorted.

Indeed, Megal had been interested immediately, and before the next match had ended, he had agreed to fund the experiment.

It had all happened so quickly. And yet, in the two years since, the doctor had made very little progress. How had Miss Trudy managed to make so much headway?

He had never met the missing enlistee. And Marilyn he'd only met once before at Megal's office. But going through line after line of Trudy's code, he felt like he did know the mysterious general. She was incredibly methodical, neat, precise. She was unlikely to turn up to a game night covered in ink. He admired her greatly.

One thing he had gleaned was that Miss Trudy's algorithm assumed that every anomaly had only one entry point and an infinity of exit points. This was novel. He had thought entry and exit points occupied the same space, that traffic could be two way. But from what he could ascertain, Miss Trudy thought that both the single entry point and the infinity of exit points were structured like one-way valves. He wasn't certain, but he thought that with enough data, the algorithm could detect the location of the valves that moved from this space into the anomaly – essentially the entry point.

He was dying to find out how the hell Miss Trudy had acquired a Thinktank; he was sure it would be a hell of a story. And how had she developed this algorithm? And how on the Two Worlds had she received the dead letter that had sent her into the anomaly at Jellicoe Street? The only way to find the answers was to find a way in himself.

Simon grabbed his ethometer from his bag. It was no Thinktank, but it had a small amount of processing power. He wondered how he could get Trudy's algorithm on to it. He had no idea if the two devices could interface and he didn't fancy hand-coding it in as he had his own algorithm. It would take days, days which Miss Trudy possibly didn't have.

He turned his ethometer on and to his surprise the Thinktank beeped. A small square appeared over the text on the frontispiece.

Connect to ethometer?

Y/N

Dr Simon pressed the Y key. The message was replaced with a new one.

Send current file to connected ethometer?

Y/N

Dr Simon stared at the letters on the screen. How on the Two Worlds could the Thinktank be connected to the ethometer without, well, a connection? There was no cable between them. That sort of technology was like something from Underworld.

He leaned forward and pressed Y on the keyboard. Both machines whirred loudly for a few seconds and flickered. Could this really work, he wondered, with growing excitement, as the Thinktank made some authoritative beeps. His ethometer responded with its own smaller beeps. And then they both went completely dead.

"Damn," he said. He looked at the two hunks of metal before him. He had killed them. A Thinktank and an ethometer, gone. He abandoned them and went to slouch on a sofa.

Simon had considered himself a scientist, a real knowledge seeker, someone who held the ideals of Overworld dear – but he'd spent two years out at the Apple Quarter testing explosives and shooting rabbits. And now, he'd killed not only his own ethometer, but also the one machine that might be able to help him find a real space/time anomaly. He was a complete failure.

He glanced at the pile of comics that sat on a side table. On top was a copy of Stargirl. He'd loved that comic as a kid. It was one of the reasons he'd gotten into science, gotten mixed up with these forgers of the future. And look where it had led him. He may as well have spent his time reading comics, like Mr Megal. And yet, Megal had made squillions in the two years since The Last War, and squillions during the wars themselves. What was in these comics then? Was Megal receiving coded messages from Stargirl that Simon had missed? He reached out for the comic book, but before he grabbed it the ethometer beeped. He looked up and saw that both it and the Thinktank had turned back on. When he went up to peer at the frontispiece of the computer, he saw there was a new message.

Transfer complete.

Dr Simon smiled and grabbed his coat.

13

Pieces of the puzzle

Marilyn didn't quite understand how or why, but it seemed that Trudy had been dispersed amongst the immediate neighbours of 12 Jellicoe Street. Eyeballs, hair, voice – all over the place. She wondered if Trudy were in pain.

"I can help you," Marilyn said again to the hunched form in front of her. "I can make things go back to how they were."

She said this instinctively; she didn't have any idea if it were true. For all she knew, the three original neighbours had been destroyed. Collateral damage. But the blind woman understood and began to shuffle forward.

"You knew I would come," Marilyn said.

"I saw you before." It was Trudy's voice but hollow and fearsome. It seemed to come from deep within the hunched over figure, but tremendously deep, as though she were bigger on the inside.

"You heard us talking to your neighbours?" Marilyn said.

"I saw you before," the woman said again. "When I had eyes to see."

Marilyn shivered. Inside the voice, she heard the unimaginable depth of the universe. She tried to block out the sound, but it resonated in her brain and she felt the sharp tang of bile at the back of her throat.

They had been making their slow way out of the house and were now on the porch. Across the road, Isabel looked over at them, shielding her eyes against the sun. She looked a little frazzled; not something Marilyn had ever expected of the confident driver. Nevertheless, she had the two Tees with her, and that was all that mattered.

"You are a part of Miss Trudy," Marilyn said to the woman.

"I am a hole of Trudy," the woman said. "But I told you this before."

They crossed the road and joined the other Trudys.

"Now what?" Isabel said, her temper obviously short.

"Now we find out what's on the other side of this fence," said Marilyn.

"What fence?" said Tee Two. "Your friend here has been going on about it too. You're all fucking barmy."

Marilyn wondered if this hostility, if this cursing came from Trudy. Certainly not the Trudy she had known. Or not known.

She guided Tee One, Tee Two and Number 13 to stand in a small circle.

"I think you need to hold hands," she said. "Get close." She hadn't meant to sound so unsure, but now that they were here, all the pieces at the very spot, it seemed unreal. Like something from Underworld – not solid Overworld knowledge, not something made of shapes and numbers, but something mysterious. She placed Number 13's right hand in Tee Two's left one, and her left hand in Tee One's right. But try as she might, she could not induce Tee Two to take Tee One's hand to close the circle.

"Of course," Marilyn thought, remembering their interactions at the house. "She can't perceive Tee One." And if she couldn't perceive Tee One then how could she hold her hand?

"We have to find another way to close the circle," Marilyn said. "It won't work if they just stand near to one another."

"I'll do it," said Isabel, moving to stand between Tee One and Tee Two.

"No, Miss Isabel," said Marilyn. "We don't know what's going to happen here and your duty is to Mr Megal. Allow me." There was no request in her voice.

"May I call you by your name?" Isabel asked.

"You may."

"It has been an honour to serve alongside you, Marilyn. I wish you the speed of the wind, the resolve of a mountain, the power of the ocean, and the spirit of fire." Isabel smiled. "An old Northern saying."

"Thank you, Isabel," Marilyn said. "The honour has been mine." She stepped into the circle, reached out and took the hands on either side of her. They were complete now, a circle of Trudys and one Marilyn. At first, nothing happened. But then she could hear a hum, as though a beehive were nearby. The hum grew louder, and she realised it was herself. She was vibrating. She was vibrating at the background sound of the universe.

"Isabel!" she called out. But then everything disappeared and she knew she was no longer in Overworld, or in any world at all.

* * *

Mr Megal eyed off the young man opposite him. Eager chap from the sort of family where none of the sisters were enlistees.

"Well," Barwell said impatiently. "Are you interested in what I know about the experiment or aren't you?"

"How do you know about it at all?" Megal asked.

Barwell waved his hand impatiently. "Now is not the time for that conversation," he said.

"But it's related?"

"Of course it's related. Everything is. That's the nature of space time. But listen, Simon's experiment, it will fail. You cannot find an anomaly with a dead letter."

"Why not?"

"One does not simply walk into an anomaly!" the young man said, raising his voice. Megal glanced over at Burton and Collins at the other table, but they were absorbed in their conversation and wine. Megal motioned to Barwell to continue.

"Simon started from a wrong assumption. He thought that anomalies would be huge, large enough to have their own address." Barwell shook his head. "The arrogance. I admit, at first, I thought so too. I blindly followed his logic that given the geography of Overworld, our dependence on geometry, an anomaly would fit a discrete space here, something we could measure. That it could be found in the Overworld Postal System directory, for the love of the Two Worlds!" Barwell gave a short laugh and shook his head again.

"But I've done more research and the fact is that there is no anomaly large enough to contain a letter, let alone a whole house. Imagine it. If you find an anomaly and use one of Simon's half-baked ideas to try to enter it, what will happen?"

Megal hadn't seen, but he knew what the others suspected about the neighbours on Jellicoe Street. The person would shatter, split into several pieces.

"Why are you telling me this now?" he said.

"I learned about your experiments just this morning," Barwell said. "Your investigations at Panko were... indiscreet."

"Yes, but why tell me at all?"

Barwell looked away then his gaze dropped to his hands on the table. "Does it matter?"

"Yes, I rather think it does," said Megal.

"I just don't want any harm to come to Simon. I... I worked with him years ago and have carried on my own calculations. When I heard that you two had met, I suspected that he had probably put one of his crazy plans into action. And when I found out that the Whiting woman was involved... I just don't want him to get hurt. Or caught up in something he doesn't understand."

"What do you know of the Whiting woman?" said Megal.

"Nothing. Nothing at all. Only by reputation. That whatever she gets involved in, always succeeds. It's one of those rumours one hears about. My grandfather was a general in the Last War But One and spoke of her."

"Whiting was in that war too?"

"Yes. And I think the Previous War, also."

"But how did you come to learn all this? How did you know she was involved with Dr Simon's experiment?"

"Like you, Mr Megal, I'm learning how to use information. We forgers of the future find and use what implements we can. I greatly admire how you expanded your fortune in the Last War without actually getting involved in it."

"I see." Megal looked more closely at the young man. His original impression hadn't changed; the lad was overeager, harried, with ink stains on his fingers and smeared across his tie. But he looked rueful, as if his life were slipping away from him in slow but sure increments. Hardly the type to make a fortune, although Megal wished him luck with it. Indeed, he reminded him of Dr Simon.

"The doctor didn't use your honorific when he spoke of you. So you're a doctor yourself?"

"Was," the young man said miserably. "Now I'm a bloody Baron."

"Oh!" Megal said. "Dr Simon didn't mention you were royalty!" Megal, rich as he was, had met very few actual aristocrats. They moved very much in their own circles. He had sometimes wondered if they weren't a fiction of Government, to appease those who had fond memories of Underworld, when princes and gods had walked the Two Worlds.

"It's an encumbrance I'd rather not have," Barwell said. "Out there… It's why I can't leave. Every movement I make is monitored. I can't even send a letter without it being tracked. My scientific experiments are over. This is the only haven I have, but it's become my prison." Barwell gave a wry smile. "While Simon looks for his anomaly, I find myself trapped in my own."

"What do you know of Miss Trudy Whiting and who she is fighting?" Megal tried again, but Barwell shook his head.

"Megal, I know nothing of all that. As I said, only rumours. Listen, Simon must first look for adjacent anomalies that could combine to form a larger one. And then he must find a way to merge them. Only then could he enter via the single entry point."

"And what would happen theoretically if a person were to enter an anomaly that were too small?"

Von Barwell paused. "Then she succeeded already?"

Megal did not reply.

"I can see no way in which she could have avoided being... Torn asunder, shall we say? If one anomaly can't contain her, well, it's only natural several would vie for the pieces."

Megal shuddered. "Could Dr Simon have known this before we started?"

The Baron looked wounded. "Oh, I cannot answer that. Space time, you know, it's not like other sciences. There's no consistency. Just because there is one small anomaly today, doesn't mean it was there yesterday, or that it was the same size or shape. But no, he started from a wrong assumption, so he could not have known. He always thought of an anomaly as a house, a palace. Whereas I think it's more like..."

"A glass of wine?" Megal said, pointing to his own.

"A thought. A wink. A teardrop."

"This is all very disturbing, Baron Doctor."

"Perhaps next time you get involved in space time, you'll be more circumspect."

"Indeed," said Mr Megal. "Well, Baron Doctor, it was a pleasure meeting you. If you have any further information, here is my card."

Barwell took the card and the two men stood.

"Are you leaving so soon?" the Baron said.

"I had better tell Dr Simon your information with haste, I think."

"Yes, of course."

Poor young man, Megal thought. *Rich young baron, but poor young man.*

Before they reached the sanctuary of the Library, the Baron grabbed Megal by the arm.

"Tell him I miss him," he said earnestly. "No. No. Don't tell him."

Megal was silent while the young man wrestled internally.

"Which is it to be, Baron Doctor?"

"Tell him I miss him," the young man said quietly, and he

withdrew back into the dining room and towards the smoking den beyond.

Megal passed back through the Library and into the Reception Hall. Isabel was probably still at Jellicoe Street, he thought, as the Undersecretary passed him his hat and cane. Ordinarily, he would walk back to Sky Tall as it was only a few blocks, but his shoes pinched and he felt tired of a sudden. He could ask for the Club Driver to take him home; may as well make the most of his membership fees.

"I say, my man," he was starting to say to the Undersecretary, when he heard a tremendous commotion outside. He and the Undersecretary looked over. There was some sort of struggle at the door, two drunk men quarrelling perhaps, and before he could quite believe it there was Isabel, wrestling the doorman through the front door and pinning him to the floor.

"Under. No. Circumstances!" the doorman gasped out while trying to heave Isabel off his prostrate form. "You. Shall. Not. Pass!"

"But I already have, mate," Isabel said, binding the doorman's hands with her scarf. The first woman to pass into that hallowed building for centuries.

"Miss Isabel!" Megal said.

"Mr Megal," she said, leaping up from the floor and taking Megal by the wrist. "We have to go. Marilyn's in danger."

14

The time traveller

Isabel had no idea what happened. She knew only this; there had been a circle of women, and then there had not. The moment Marilyn's hands had reached out to take the others' hands, they had all completely vanished.

"It worked," she said, but she wasn't entirely sure what 'it' was. Presumably, Marilyn was now wherever Trudy was and the two of them would find a way out. Isabel picked her hat up from the ground and began to fan herself with it. What was she to do in the meantime? She could go back to Sky Tall Building and see what the doc had figured out. And there was the envelope which Marilyn had left at that ratty house.

"Dammit," she said aloud. She'd quite liked being in a duo. It was good to have a buddy. Much better than sitting alone all day in Megal's reception room, hoping against hope that something interesting would happen. And it had! But now she was all alone again.

"Dammit!" she said, this time quite loudly, and crushed her hat in her hand. She immediately regretted this and started to pull it back into shape and to dust the dirt off the brim. How had it got so damn dusty? Isabel beat at it, then paused and thought back. Why had her hat been on the ground? She hadn't taken it off while they'd been standing around the fence waiting for Marilyn and the creature across the road, and she didn't think she'd taken it off as they'd formed their haphazard circle. It must have been knocked off somehow, although she had no memory of it.

"Damn. *It!*" she said. She had lost memories! How on the Two Worlds had that happened? She never forgot a thing. She checked her watch. She couldn't remember exactly when she had checked it last, but she thought that perhaps she had lost about an hour. She sniffed the air carefully. Yes, it was starting to smell like mid-afternoon and it had definitely still smelled like morning before.

Well, this at least she knew how to deal with. She knew perfectly well how to recover memories.

Isabel closed her eyes and thought back to the few seconds before Marilyn had closed the circle. She breathed carefully, thinking of the smells she had noticed and the ones she had ignored. The bodies of the women, the broken grass beneath their feet, a passing bird, the still warm car. Yes. Here it was. She was close now.

Just as the circle had closed, the whole world had shivered. It was this that had knocked her hat off. And suddenly, sharply, she could smell something she could never have expected. It was Marilyn; it was fear.

"Isabel!" Marilyn had cried out.

Isabel snapped her eyes open and sprinted to the Cab.

"I'm coming, Marilyn!" she yelled out as she gunned it into motion. "Hold tight, enlistee, I'm on my way!"

* * *

MEGAL AND ISABEL dashed out of the elevator in Megal's basement and collided with Dr Simon.

"Welcome," the doctor said.

"Tell me you've got something, doc," Isabel said.

"I've got something," the doctor dutifully replied.

There was a short pause.

"Doc, were you just being funny?"

"Ahem," Dr Simon said. "No, of course not. I mean, a little. But I have actually got something."

"Great," Isabel said. "You can tell us about it on the way. Take everything you need. Everything. I don't want any more delays. We take our complete arsenal and we fight until this is over."

"Yes, ma'am," said the doctor. He held up his ethometer, indicating he was completely ready. Within 120 seconds of arriving, Isabel and Megal were leaving the Sky Tall basement, with the doctor in tow.

At ground level, they were met by a burly woman dressed in canvas overalls wearing strong-looking leather gloves that reached her elbows.

"Miss Helena!" Isabel said with a smile. She turned to the two men. "Gentlemen, Miss Helena will be your driver for the remainder of the day. Let's go." They made their way to the Cab which Isabel had left parked on the street. Helena took the wheel. Isabel sat in front and turned to face the men in the back as the Cab took off.

"Gentlemen, listen up."

As they drove across the City, she explained as succinctly as she could what had happened at Jellicoe Street.

When she got to the part where she had lost her memories, Dr Simon let out a cry.

"What is it, doc?"

"How much? How much time did you lose?" he said, excited.

"I can't be exactly sure," Isabel said. "I think less than an hour, but more than 30 minutes."

"A time pop," he said. "Miss Isabel, you didn't lose those minutes. You travelled through them!"

"What do you mean?"

"When an anomaly is created, there is sudden displacement of time. I call it a time pop," Simon said. "Although I did also consider calling it a time wave. What do you think?"

"So Marilyn created another anomaly?" Isabel said.

"Not created," Megal said. "Merged."

Dr Simon looked at him. "What do you mean?" he asked.

"According to your friend, the Baron Doctor von Barwell, your experiments will fail because there is no anomaly large enough to contain an object, not even a dead letter, and certainly not a person. That would have been good to know *before* we sent a person into one, I think. And now two people."

"Barry knew?" Dr Simon said. "But how? He started with the same assumptions as me."

Megal shook his head. "Seems we weren't the only ones working on this little problem. Not by a long shot. Also, he misses you."

"So I travelled through time, doc?" Isabel interrupted.

"He what?" Simon said. "Oh. Yes, Miss Isabel, you did. You may now call yourself a time traveller."

"The Baron thought it was ridiculous to assume that an anomaly would adhere to our geometry," Megal said. He had taken off his jacket and tie and undone the top two buttons of his shirt. The skin underneath was flushed and pink. "There was never one anomaly. There were many small ones."

"I don't care how many anomalies there were," Isabel said. "Listen, gents, you're going to carry on to Jellicoe Street. Miss Helena here will take care of you. And you, doc, are going to use your ethometer or any other damn mojo you happen to possess and you are going to open up that damn portal or anomaly, and rescue Miss Marilyn and whatever is left of Miss Trudy. You get them out of there if you have to beat the damn door down. Because I don't know anything about space folds or time pops but I know fear when I smell it. And Miss Marilyn is afraid."

The Cab drew to a stop and Isabel got out. "In the meantime, I'm going to chase down the envelope and see what we can find. I'll meet you fellows back at Jellicoe Street in a jiffy."

"We could just wait for you," said Dr Simon.

"No!" Isabel said firmly. "You go back there and you get Miss Marilyn out. Do you understand me?"

"Yes, ma'am," said Megal. Isabel shut the door and Helena didn't wait before roaring off in the Cab so fast that the men were thrust back into their seats.

15

Fractures and fractals

"These enlistees!" Dr Simon said, raising his voice against the roar of the engine. "Where do you find them?"

Megal waved his hand as if to say, not now, man!

"Explain to me about these anomalies," he said. "According to the Baron Doctor, it's not possible for an anomaly to contain a letter, so how could it contain a whole house?"

"Oh yes," said Dr Simon. "You see, one plus one plus one never equals three in an anomaly. Oh! I rhymed! Marvellous." The doctor's face lit up with delight.

"Dr Simon, I am only going to say this once," said Megal quietly, leaning very close to him. "You have so far known me to be a kind and generous man. But I am the CEO and owner of Megal Enterprises. Under my direction, we have expanded into 55 districts and I now own one third of the property in the City. Let me assure you, this was not by being kind and generous. I am concerned and a little worried about the situation we have found ourselves in, a situation that you should have known more about. You do not want me to be worried or concerned, Dr Simon. Unpleasant things happen to other people when I am worried or concerned. Do you understand me?"

Dr Simon had been looking down at his hands in his lap during this speech. "I do," he said. "Very clearly."

"Then tell me again about the maths."

"Of course," said the doctor, and his voice was no longer playful. "So when an anomaly collides or merges with another anomaly, it's not like adding. Two lots of one-centimetre anomalies don't make a two-centimetre anomaly. It's more like exponentiation."

"To what power?"

"I'm not sure. It depends on the factor of time. Which is what we may be able to glean from Miss Isabel's lost time. And what we know about the current size of the anomaly."

"Which is?"

"Mr Megal!" said the doctor, forgetting himself. "It's the size of the house!"

"But this is what I don't understand," said Megal. "If the anomalies are all small, what happened to number 12 Jellicoe Street?"

"It was subsumed by the anomaly," Dr Simon said.

"But you said all the anomalies are small!"

"Oh, no, it wasn't subsumed by those! By this one."

"Which one?"

"12 Jellicoe Street was subsumed by the anomaly created when the three smaller anomalies merged."

"But that only happened today," said Megal. "The house has been missing for at least several days."

"Ah, basic space time error," said the doctor, forgetting himself again. "The larger anomaly expanded in all four directions. In space and in time."

"Wait," Megal said. "So what you're saying is that by merging the anomalies today, Miss Marilyn created the larger anomaly that subsumed the house in the past, which is how Miss Trudy was able to receive the dead letter and be transported into the smaller anomalies and be separated into three parts in the first place?"

"Exactly," said Dr Simon with a grin.

"But if the large anomaly existed then, when did the three anomalies exist?"

"Oh, Mr Megal," said Dr Simon. "They existed before the large one was formed."

Dr Simon continued to shake his head, muttering to himself about basic space time maths and didn't they teach the right things in schools anymore?

As she drew the car to a stop in Jellicoe Street, Helena turned to the two men, but said nothing. They got out and stood in the side yard of number 14, where Marilyn had gathered the Tees.

"Well, let's see if Miss Trudy's algorithm worked," said Dr Simon, and he took out his ethometer. The moment he switched it on, it let out loud screeching noises.

Megal covered his ears. "What is it?" he yelled out.

"No idea," Dr Simon said, and quickly shut it off. He looked at the two houses to their left and right and headed towards number ten. "Let's try somewhere where the signal isn't as strong so I can make adjustments." Just past the other side of the house, where he knew for certain the anomaly wasn't, he switched on the ethometer, and again it began to screech.

Dr Simon moved the device around, up, down, left, right, and still it let out its horrible noise. On the road, on the lawn, near the house, it didn't matter. Nothing could lessen the noise coming from the machine, except to turn it off.

The doctor sat down heavily on the grass.

"I don't understand," he said. "I calculated every variable. I input the data from the time pop, the physical size from the land survey, every blasted bit of information we have wrangled about this damn anomaly and I can't find the entry point. There's just too much interference. Miss Trudy was right. They are everywhere."

"The anomalies?" said Megal, standing over him with his arms crossed.

"Yes! They're everywhere. Absolutely everywhere."

"You're not looking for just any anomaly," said a deep voice. The two men turned to see Helena standing near them. "You are looking for one that used to be three."

"Yes, of course," said Dr Simon, with a sigh. Was he to be schooled on everything, by every woman, enlistee and chauffeur that he met?

"What do you do when you're driving down a street and you're looking for a particular address?" the driver said.

"What? I don't know. I don't drive," said Dr Simon.

"You turn down the radio," Helena said.

Dr Simon looked up at her. "I need to turn down the background noise. All right. But how?"

"An anomaly formed by three smaller ones will have a different resonant frequency," Helena said. "No exponentiation without autocorrelation."

Dr Simon smacked his head and started tapping wildly on the ethometer. "By the Two Worlds, you're absolutely right, Miss Helena. You study fractal dimensions?"

"I dabble," she said with a shrug. She reached a hand down to help him to his feet.

"Thank you very much," he said. He turned on the ethometer and it let out a low buzz. He breathed out audibly. "Excellent. Let's go find us an entry point."

In the side yard, Dr Simon carefully swung his ethometer back and forth in a regular sweep. Helena stood watching him, arms crossed, her face unreadable. Megal stood by anxiously, tapping out a tattoo on the fence. Once, he moved aside so Simon could scan the spot where he stood, and the doctor lingered there so long that Megal finally became irritated.

"Well, man, what is it?"

"You seem to have found the spot," Dr Simon said. He was still peering at his ethometer, but he looked up with a smile. "Here it is." He was pointing at a spot on the fence, the exact place where Megal had been tapping.

"This is the front door. This is the way in. Now we just need to find a key." He began to fiddle with the ethometer again.

"Let's just knock the damn thing down," Megal said, slapping the fence. "Isn't that what Miss Isabel told us to do?"

"You could try that," Isabel said, coming up to them from the road. "Or how about an invitation?" In her hands, she was holding an envelope.

16

A cottage in Encyc

Isabel knocked on the door of the dingy cottage in Encyc, and waited for several agonising minutes, before it was opened by a tall young Black woman.

"Yes?" the woman said, wedging her shoulder against the door.

"My name is Isabel. I'm here about the envelope that Marilyn left behind."

The woman stared at Isabel, her black eyes unblinking, the tip of her tongue just visible between her teeth.

"And who are you?" she asked. Isabel felt her looking down at her, taking in her hat, her prim yellow dress, her neat driving gloves.

"I work with Marilyn," Isabel said.

"Marilyn's retired," the woman said. "Full pension. So who are you really?"

"I'm a friend," Isabel said. "I think you can tell that, can't you? This morning, Marilyn dropped off an envelope at this house to be examined. I need to know what you've found out. It's imperative I get that envelope."

"Listen here, miss, I don't know you, and I certainly don't take orders from -"

"No, you listen," Isabel said. "Marilyn is missing. I have to find her. And this envelope is part of it."

The woman stared at her but said nothing.

"I know what you're doing here," Isabel said, sniffing the air slightly. "And I have no interest in it. It's not illegal and even if it were, I wouldn't care. I only care about Marilyn. And I'm guessing you do too. So please, the envelope. It's my best chance of finding her."

"You can smell it, huh?" the young woman said.

Isabel nodded.

"Yeah," the woman said. "Well, I can taste it."

Isabel grimaced. "Oh, I'm sorry," she said.

"Don't be sorry. It's my damn business. And as you said, it isn't anything illegal. Let's get out of here."

The woman stepped outside the cottage, drawing the door firmly shut behind her. She gestured for Isabel to follow her around the corner, down another street lined with leather and iron shops.

"I can tell you're not trouble," the woman said. "A nice well-brought up girl like you, and you didn't call Marilyn 'Miss'. You must be really close."

"We have been through some… stuff," Isabel said.

"Yeah, haven't we all," said the woman. "So this thing with the envelope and Miss M; is it some kind of weird joke?"

"No, I assure you, she's missing. But I am doing everything I can to find her and bring her back."

"I'm not worried about Miss M. She goes missing and comes back all the time. This won't be any different. But the envelope."

"What?" said Isabel. "Do you know where it came from?"

"Thing is, it didn't take me two minutes to crack it. I just couldn't do it right when she came in, told her it would have to wait a few hours. Maybe I should have just damn well looked at it as soon as she came." The young woman paused at a play park made up mostly of cracked concrete and broken iron. She pulled the envelope out of the pocket of her dark leather jacket. She stared at it for a moment and then handed it to Isabel.

It was a perfectly normal envelope, brown and mottled, with the

Jellicoe address clearly written on the front in neat lower-class handwriting. There was no return address on the back.

"See, the writing isn't hers," said the young woman, pointing to the address. "M's got that flowery boarding school script, probably like what you've got." She flipped the envelope to show the seal. "But I'd know that taste anywhere. It was Merry. Merry sent this letter."

Isabel shook her head. "But who is Merry?"

"Merry," said the woman. "My sister. Merry Lynn."

"Marilyn?" said Isabel, dumbfounded. "Marilyn sent this envelope?"

The woman nodded. "Yep. Sure as day. She didn't write it, but she definitely sent it. I'd say about four or five days ago, so I don't know how she could have forgotten already."

"Because she hasn't done it yet," Isabel said. "Now where can I find a reliable driver?"

17

An enlistee and a General

When the world stopped buzzing, Marilyn was able to open her eyes. The three neighbours from Jellicoe Street and Isabel had disappeared. As had the street, the fence, the houses, the lawn. Wherever she was, she was alone.

As her eyes were still adjusting to whatever this space was, she immediately strained her ears. Nothing. It was like she was in an acoustically dead room.

Or a vacuum.

With a start, Marilyn realised that there was nothing wrong with her vision. She was just in complete emptiness. There was nothing around her, nothing to see, nothing to hear, nothing to measure anything against, nothing whatsoever. All around her was the beige of the universe. Even her own black skin was muted, blending in with the background colour.

She had never been so alone in her entire life.

"Calm, Merry," she said out loud. Her voice seemed to disappear as it left her mouth. "You've got oxygen, at least. Or some way of breathing."

She reached out one tentative foot and then the other. She could feel no ground beneath her feet, but she was compelled to move, although she had the impression that whether she tried to move or stay still was all one and the same in this space. But somewhere in this vast emptiness was a woman who could tell her what the hell was going on, and hopefully get them both out.

Marilyn had fought brutal battles, had seen unspeakable acts of cruelty. She had served proudly in the Last War and was not afraid to serve again if Overworld needed her to. But this empty place, so dense and yet full of nothingness, scared her. Moving without the sense of moving, walking on nothing, going from nowhere to nowhere else.

It was pointless, futile. And yet it was her life now. It was all she had.

She pushed on.

After what might have been a year, or a minute, or a day, or an hour, she perceived a change around her. A darkening to the beige, a hint of a breeze in the stillness.

"Miss Trudy," she called out, and she felt that her voice travelled further than before. "It's Marilyn."

There was no answer. The nothingness was still too dense. She carried on, metres or kilometres, minutes or days, until again she could perceive a change.

"Trudy!" she called out, and this time she felt her voice go beyond her, felt it penetrate the emptiness. "Trudy! Show yourself!"

Marilyn felt all the beige around her gathering and pulling together. Her hat started to vibrate and she took it from her head and clutched it against her chest. The whole space around was swirling and twirling, spinning faster and faster and growing in intensity. She felt like she was in the centre of a vortex. She could hear a rushing in her ears that was more than wind, that was more than the storm. It seemed to be the universe screaming, screaming directly into her brain.

And then she heard it. She heard what the universe was screaming.

"Marilyn!" it called out to her. "Marilyn!"

Marilyn stood up as tall as she could, let the wind buffet her as much as it might, and she screamed back.

"Come and get me!"

* * *

THEY WERE in a perfectly normal lounge room. Trudy was standing in the centre, wearing the same suit she had worn so long ago, and yet just three days ago, in the Office of Dead Letters.

"Miss Marilyn," she said dully. "How lovely to see you."

Marilyn looked about at the common furniture, the ordinary rug. But outside the window, she could see nothing but beige. "Yes," she said. "Lovely to see you too. Where are we?"

Trudy glanced about. "Well, I assume that this must be number 12 Jellicoe Street."

"But you're not sure?"

"I only just arrived," Trudy said. "Why? What is it?"

"Well, it's only…" Marilyn said. "You've been gone for three days."

Trudy made a slight grimace. "I've been out there for three days," she said, waving towards the window. "But you found me. You brought me here."

"Of course," said Marilyn. "That's what I was employed to do."

"You were not employed," said Trudy. "You were engaged to open letters. Nothing more."

"As were you," said Marilyn. "Or so I thought."

"Ah yes, you've been busy, I gather," Trudy said. She smiled wanly and sat on one of the modular sofas. She looked tired. "Three days, you said?"

"It was three days after you disappeared that I entered the anomaly. But I don't know how much time has passed since then. I felt I was out in that for a long time, but it was impossible to measure."

"Either way, a long time to have my particles spread across the universe."

"Not so long in universal terms," Marilyn said tartly and she sat on the sofa opposite. "Well, then, haven't you turned out to be quite the surprise."

Trudy raised her eyebrows. "I don't think I was so much of an enigma."

"You had me fooled, and let me tell you that is no small matter."

"Simple misdirection."

Marilyn huffed. "You certainly always seemed very innocuous. And yet there you were with a Thinktank in your kitchen."

"Ah, so you found that then. Of course." Trudy paused. "But you didn't get chlorinated?"

Marilyn looked momentarily guarded, then she smiled and wiggled her fingers. "Touch," she said. "I could feel your password."

"Oh!" Trudy said. "*Nice.*"

"Hm," Marilyn said. She stood and circled the room a few times and each time she passed the window, she looked away. She reached out and touched the walls, brushed her fingers along the mantel, gripped the sofa, tapped against the wooden furnishings. She knew that this was 12 Jellicoe Street, that this house had once been in her own world, in Overworld, sitting real and physically between numbers 10 and 14 Jellicoe Street. But it felt like nothing. Whoever had lived here – their name had forever been erased from the Overworld Postal System directory and every other official document – their memories too had been made nonexistent. Whoever had painted that wall, plumped that pillow, shut that cupboard door for the final time not only didn't exist, but had never existed.

On the third circuit, Marilyn forced herself to stop and look out – at the beige, that unending dead zone that contained all the life in the universe.

"Miss Trudy, tell me. Where are we? Why are we here? And how do we get out?"

"I think we are past honorifics, Marilyn." Trudy stood up from the sofa and moved to stand by her colleague at the window. "You know who I am."

"Yes."

"Then believe me when I tell you that I have one goal and one goal only: to stop the war. That is why we are here."

"You were Philosophy Division. Did you know about the experiment before you were engaged by Mr Megal?"

Trudy looked surprised. "You have done your homework. Yes, I was familiar with the theories before I joined. And the moment I started working at the Office, I knew I could crack it before that useless doctor. And I did, didn't I? I cracked it."

The words sat between them uncomfortably. Marilyn hated it here, in this quiet dead place and she began to pace again. The floors did not creak, there were no creatures scurrying in the eaves, branches did not brush against the windows. There was no wind, no life. She sat on the sofa, but could not feel it. The rug beneath her feet had no history. The very floors and walls were dead, dead, dead.

"Don't you know what happened?" Marilyn said.

"No," Trudy admitted. "Not really. Not at all, actually." She gave a short sharp laugh.

"The anomaly was too small to contain you," Marilyn said.

Trudy nodded. "More correctly, the anomaly didn't exist yet?"

"That's right. You were split across three smaller anomalies. Across three of the neighbours of this house. They each became a manifestation of you."

"Ha!" said Trudy. "No, they became manifestations of the anomalies. That must have looked interesting. And so? How did you merge them?"

"I simply brought them together."

"And you came with them? Why?"

"They couldn't close the circle on their own."

Trudy was nodding. "Yes, yes. And then when they merged, the large anomaly was created and I was able to manifest here. In Jellicoe Street."

"Where were you before?" said Marilyn.

"Everywhere," said Trudy. "In all places at once. I have felt the whole of creation in my atoms."

"Sounds incredible," said Marilyn.

"I'm not so sure."

Marilyn stood up and went over to Trudy. "General First Order

Trudy Grayling, I have devoted the past three days to finding you. I have found you. Now, I must ask you: do you require assistance to exit this situation?"

At this, Trudy laughed. She actually laughed. "Never rescue anyone who doesn't need rescuing, hey?"

"One of the first rules we learn," Marilyn said. "And I'm looking at you, and where you are, and how you got here, and I'm starting to think that you don't want to leave. After all this, you only just arrived."

"You're incredibly smart," Trudy said. "Mr Megal was right to engage you. Yes, I'm exactly where I want to be, where I need to be. I have a mission to carry out."

"To stop the war?"

"To stop the war."

Marilyn looked out the window briefly, but turned away from it and leaned against the wall next to Trudy.

"But the war is over. We won. Overworld won."

"Did we?" said Trudy. "Yes, we separated ourselves finally from Underworld. The geography has changed and it can't go back. But is this what we fought for? So men like Mr Megal could have everything? And those who live in Panko have almost nothing?"

Marilyn stared at Trudy. It was the sort of speech she expected her sister to make, not a General First Order.

"We can change it," Trudy said quietly. "We don't have to lose our values to win the war. We can find a better solution."

"If you stop the war, isn't that rather putting yourself out of a job, General?"

"I wouldn't wish for war for all the stars in the universe," Trudy said angrily. "If you'd seen what I've seen, enlistee…"

"I have," said Marilyn.

Trudy paused. "You have," she said. "We all saw too much."

"Whose side are you on?"

"You're asking the wrong questions," Trudy said. "If you mean am I fighting for Overworld, the answer is yes. I always fight for Overworld and for our people. I don't long for Underworld or its ways. I fight *for* Overworld, always."

"So where do you intend to go? Or when?"

"That I don't know yet," Trudy said. "Unfortunately, this happened unexpectedly. I wasn't supposed to be delivered with the letter. I was hoping to learn of the location of an anomaly, not get dragged inside, too. I need my research, but I can't leave, and I can't figure out how to leave without my research." She paused and then went back over to the sofa and sat heavily. "I don't suppose you have an ethometer?"

18

The arrival of the cavalry

At the fence between numbers 10 and 14 Jellicoe Street, there were gathered four people. Two white men, one tall and ginger, the other medium and brown. The two women were also white, one pale and slight, the other burly and strong. They knew unequivocally that they were in the right place. They just had no idea what to do next.

Megal was standing still, very still, and Isabel eyed him warily. She had never known him to be so quiet, so motionless. Movement came as naturally to him as breathing; he was constantly in motion. He strolled, he walked, he tapped, he shook, but he rarely just stood.

Dr Simon was shaking his head. "I just don't know. Between the ethometer and the envelope, sure, I guess we should be able to get in. But I just don't know how."

Suddenly, Megal ran at the fence and smashed his shoulder into it.

"Arrrrgh!" he yelled out, as the fence swayed but did not give. "Arrrgh!" he yelled again. Dr Simon stepped back in shock and Helena gave a broad grin. But Isabel went to Megal and placed her hand on his shoulder.

"Mr Megal," she said, before he could take another charge at the fence.

"We must do something!" he said.

"Mr Megal," Isabel said again. "If you want to knock down the fence, by all means, let's knock down the fence. But we do it together."

"No, you fucking don't," came a voice.

They all turned to see a woman standing on the porch of the house at number 14. Isabel started. She was not the same woman she had previously met at 14 Jellicoe Street, but she was sort of similar. Sort of her, but sort of not.

"Tee?" Isabel said, striding forward.

"Tee what?" the woman said.

"Sorry, I thought we'd met before."

"Is that why you think it's okay to tramp all over my lawn? Climb over my fence? Slam into it and try to knock it down?"

"This fence?" Isabel said. "The one joining number 12?"

"There is no number 12," the woman said. "The one joining number 10, I mean. Anyway, it doesn't fucking matter. Stop vandalising my property and get the fuck off my lawn."

"I say," said Dr Simon.

Mr Megal came to stand by Isabel's side.

"Miss, my name is Mr Megal and I am the CEO and owner of Megal Enterprises. I will give you $5000 right now to knock down this fence. Miss Isabel, here is my cheque book."

"That is not necessary, Mr Megal," Isabel whispered to him.

"Deal," said the neighbour at number 14. "For 5k, you can do whatever the fuck you like."

Isabel grumbled as she took the cheque over to the woman. But walking up the porch steps, she could see just how different the woman now looked. She was the same size and shape, but her face was even, both of her eyes large and brown, all traces of Trudy erased.

"I'll need your full name," Isabel said, leaning against the banister with the cheque and a pen.

"Miss Felicity Aberystwyth," the woman said, watching carefully as Isabel wrote it down. "So is that really Mr Megal?"

"It is," Isabel said.

"You lot must be up to something damn interesting then."

"I would suggest that for $5000, it's no longer any of your business," Isabel said, handing her the cheque.

The woman shrugged and took it. "Whatever." And she went back inside.

Back at the fence, Isabel could have struck Megal.

"You damn fool," she said. He looked astonished.

"Excuse me?"

"We don't need to knock down the fence. Think about it. Why did the letter get delivered but not the envelope?"

"The letter is the object," said Dr Simon. "The envelope is just the vessel."

Helena scoffed. "Since when is an envelope not an object?" she said.

"I think the envelope is still in transit," Isabel said. "Once the letter was delivered, the envelope knew that *we* would deliver it. And here we are."

"What do you suggest?" said Megal.

"We knock," said Isabel.

19

An envelope and two empty cups

"What the hell was that?" Trudy said, as the house shook around them.

"I suspect the cavalry is trying to arrive," Marilyn said.

Trudy quickly left the room and walked down the hallway, Marilyn following after her. Through the open front door they could see nothing but cosmic latte. They stepped onto the porch and felt themselves surrounded, suffocated by the pure unending nothingness of it all.

"There," said Trudy. Marilyn looked where she was pointing. To the left of the house, breaking the inexorable beige, was a slip of colour.

"Something has broken through," Trudy said.

Marilyn leaned forward over the porch. She loathed the idea of going down the steps and back into the nothingness. What if she never made it back to the house again? But even from the porch, she could tell what the little smudge of colour was.

"That's the envelope," she said with a rare smile. "Isabel's here."

"Mr Megal's assistant?"

"You know her?"

"Of her. Very impressive service record for someone so young. Well, shall we take a look at what she has brought us?"

The two women made their way very gingerly down the steps, holding close to the banister. It's not that it was hard to move through the beige in any physical sense; but it was overpowering, somehow. It made them feel dense, woolly-headed.

"It makes you lose your senses," Marilyn said. She couldn't smell or hear anything. The banister beneath her hand was making contact with her skin, but it returned no pressure, felt utterly immaterial, like holding a ghost. She had no sense of its composition, its temperature, its history. It was chilling.

At the last step they stopped and looked at each other. There was no ground; just beige. Without a word, Trudy took Marilyn's hand and nodded. They stepped out into the void and landed on… Nothing. And on nothingness and through nothingness they walked, Marilyn casting her gaze back at the house periodically to make sure it didn't disappear.

They moved warily towards the splash of colour. Without any relational objects, it was impossible to tell how far away it was. But after a dozen or so steps they were upon it and they peered to take a closer look.

"I wonder if they can hear us out there," Marilyn said. "Hello! Isabel! Mr Megal! Dr Simon!"

They could see now that it was a narrow tunnel formed by the rolled-up envelope.

"Hey Maz!" came Isabel's voice, her hazel eye through the paper tunnel very bright.

"An ethometer," Marilyn said, without introduction. "We need one. Can you pass it through?"

"Yes, ma'am." Isabel called out something behind her that Marilyn couldn't hear. A moment later, her eye reappeared at the circle. "I've got the ethometer, but I don't know if I can make this hole any bigger."

Marilyn looked at the perfect roundness of the circle made by the envelope. It looked like Isabel had simply slid the envelope into the anomaly. If she pulled it out again, would it disappear? Would they lose their chance?

"Let me try something," Marilyn said. She reached out to touch the edge of the envelope and was surprised to discover that it was solid, actually real. She felt a wave of relief go through her to feel that it had history. On the envelope, she could sense Isabel, and her sister, and the countless unknown people who had sorted it, handled it, delivered it. "How long have I been gone?" she said.

"Only a few hours," Isabel said.

Marilyn shook her head. She had aged years, she could feel it. She reached again for the envelope and this time tried to feel the space where paper met the edge of the universe. She closed her eyes. She could feel the envelope with great intensity, contrasted against the absolute nothingness of the beige. But then she remembered that the beige wasn't nothingness; it was everything, just very spread out. She concentrated on the beige, feeling for just one atom of matter, two atoms, and pinching her fingers together like she was picking up a tissue, she carefully tugged at the universe and pulled it aside. The envelope fell inside the anomaly and landed at her feet.

"Quick," Marilyn called through the gap. "The ethometer!"

But Isabel was already thrusting it through and Trudy grabbed it.

"Good work, enlistee," Marilyn said.

"We lost our key," Isabel said. "Can you pass it back?" But try as she might, Marilyn could not get the envelope to pass back through to normal space.

"One way," said the doctor, appearing at the gap. "One way in, infinity ways out. Will you be able to get out now with the ethometer?"

Marilyn turned to look at Trudy. She was tapping at the instrument with a frown on her plain white face.

"Trudy, do we need anything else? To exit?" Marilyn said.

"What? No, this is all we need. I'd love to have my research, but that will have to wait until you return."

"Until I what?" said Marilyn.

"You can let go now," said Trudy, waving one hand absently toward her.

Marilyn turned back to the hole in the universe. Her fingers ached from holding it open but she didn't want to let go. She gazed out at the colour, the green of the grass, the blue of the sky, the hazel of Isabel's eyes.

"Thank you for everything, Isabel," Marilyn said. "I'll be going now."

"Don't be afraid," Isabel whispered to her. "Your sister told me. It's you who sends the letter."

Marilyn found that she couldn't say anything. She simply nodded, let go of her hold, and the hole in the universe closed up. She was once again surrounded by beige, nothing but beige.

"This is great," Trudy said. Marilyn looked at the general. She was peering at the ethometer closely. "The doctor's copied over my exact algorithm. This is better than I could have hoped."

"And what did you hope?" Marilyn said. "How did you expect to get out again?"

"Well, I didn't expect to be delivered!" said Trudy. "I don't know how you found me but I am damn glad that you did. Can't be good for your atoms, being scattered across the universe like that, for so long. But it would have been an eternity without you."

They walked back through the beige to the house and sat on the porch. Now that she had felt it, Marilyn wasn't quite as afraid of the unending universe, but it still made her feel empty.

"Look here," Trudy said. "With the ethometer, we can detect where and when in the universe each of these points is."

"What do you mean?"

"This isn't just beige. This is the entire universe spread out around us.

"Yes," Marilyn said. "I was able to feel the atoms. That's what I clung on to to pull the gap wider."

"Not just atoms," Trudy said. "Every point in space and time is here, somewhere."

"Out here is… Everything? So why does it feel like nothing?"

"Normal space time confusion," said Trudy. "Something spread out over infinity looks a lot like nothing."

"And the house?" Marilyn said.

"Ah, yes," Trudy said, turning to look at it. "This is actually 12 Jellicoe Street. I guess it came with me."

"With the doctor's ethometer, you can locate any point in time and space?" Trudy nodded. "And when you do, how do we open the anomaly? Once we find the right spot, how do we exit?"

"I believe you simply push through," said Trudy.

"Just push?"

"Just push."

Marilyn lifted up her hand and extended her index finger. Slowly, she pushed against the nothingness, searching, as she had before, for something to push against.

Nothing happened.

"Well, maybe you need to push harder," said Trudy. "We have all the time in the world. We'll figure it out. I wonder if there's food?"

Marilyn reached out again and closed her eyes. She thought of Isabel's voice telling her to concentrate, and she regulated her breathing. She let go of the fear that had dogged her since she'd arrived in the cosmic latte. She let go of everything and for a moment she just *was*. No feeling, no body, no senses. Only breath. Only calmness.

And as she sank into this emptiness, she felt a tiny dot of pressure begin to burn at the end of each of her fingertips. It was like what she had felt before, when she had pinched the universe, but now that she knew it was a moment in space time, and not simply an atom, she could feel them everywhere, against every single cell of her skin, all up her arms, on her legs, her neck, pressing against her face. She concentrated her senses to the tip of her index finger, focusing her sense of touch, and she felt the point begin to open…

"Marilyn!" Trudy called out. Marilyn opened her eyes and saw a glow at her fingertip.

"Where is that?" she asked.

Trudy held the ethometer to Marilyn's finger and studied the screen.

"Centuries ago. Somewhere in Blueland."

Marilyn dropped her hand and the glow disappeared but she still felt all the points of possibility pressing against her skin. Instead of being too empty, the beige now felt too full. She shook her head, smoothed out her clothes, looked up at Trudy.

"And you think you can find exactly where we need to go somewhere in all this?" Marilyn said. "'Somewhere in Blueland centuries ago' is not very precise."

"Don't you worry, enlistee. I'll get you out exactly where you need to go. Just give me some time."

"As you said, we have all the time in the world."

Later, they sat in the kitchen holding cups without tea; there wasn't any, and if there had been it wouldn't have tasted of anything. But they felt awkward sitting there so Trudy had laughingly supplied them with the empty cups.

"Almost like old times," she said, handing Marilyn a mug with a floral print.

"Hm," Marilyn said.

"How I missed that sound," Trudy said, pretending to take a sip. She looked over the top of the cup, blew away imaginary steam. "This is me now," Trudy said. "Me and the letter, we're keeping the anomaly stable. If I exit, it will collapse. I can't leave."

"Of course you can," Marilyn said, with a shake of her head.

"Well, of course I *can*," said Trudy. "You always this damn literal? You know I still have a mission. And with your little party trick -" she mimicked Marilyn pushing a hole in the universe. "You can come and go as you please, bring me what I need, help me to stop the war."

Marilyn didn't answer. She had no desire to ever return to this place. And she wasn't sure she had any desire to go back and prevent the wars. They were over now, that's what was important. They had known peace this past few years like never before. Yes, the geography had changed, and many lives had been lost. But Overworld was finally stable and free. She was keen to return to her own time and space, to a world with sounds and smells and, above all, feeling. People and places with history, some of it very new, but a lot of it still very old. She wanted to close the Office of Dead Letters and retire with the not insignificant amount of money she had accumulated over the course of the experiment.

"Think about it," Trudy said, and she went back outside to keep searching for the place and time where Marilyn would be able to exit.

20

Forward to the past

In a bottom drawer in the kitchen, Marilyn found some paper and an envelope. She fetched a pen from her satchel and paused. Funny that the very paper that would destroy 12 Jellicoe Street was to be found in the very house. She wondered if that violated some dimensional law but then imagined Dr Simon shaking his head and saying, "Basic space time error."

She tapped the pen against her teeth for a few moments, wondering what to write.

"Hello," she wrote. "There is a stunning blue dress in your wardrobe. I would like to know its story one day."

She didn't sign it, but simply folded it and stuck it in the envelope. She licked and sealed it and thrust it in her satchel, leaving the address empty. She didn't know whose writing was on the envelope, but she knew it wasn't hers.

Marilyn returned to the porch at the front of the house but there was no sign of Trudy. She called out but her voice didn't travel far and she wasn't surprised when there was no response. She sat on the steps, hopeful that Trudy would be able to find her own way back from wherever she was *out there*.

Marilyn was an Overworld woman through and through. She

genuinely believed in the ideals of Overworld, of education, of knowledge, of progress. That's why she had enlisted the moment she could. She didn't wait to be recruited; it was in her, the need to serve for her people and their ideals. When her sister had expressed sympathy for Underworld, she had understood. They were all citizens of the Two Worlds. But when Agnetha had become a passive resistor, refusing to have anything to do with the separation of Underworld, she had felt deep shame. How could her sister be so traitorous to Overworld? It's why she had served several tours, taking another two missions after her first four had passed. But what Trudy was doing, fighting her own private war – wasn't that a very Underworld thing to do? She wasn't following their careful rules, their protocols, the ones they had fought so hard for. Should Marilyn really let her stay here, in the anomaly, waging that private war?

But then again, Marilyn thought, Trudy had said she could only exit once. After that, the anomaly would collapse. Maybe Trudy would find another anomaly, but she couldn't count on that. Once you have the strongest position, you don't give it up easily, Marilyn knew. Trudy would stay exactly where she was, trapped in her cosmic latte jail, until she found the exact moment to emerge, to carry out her mission and stop the war. If Trudy were any sort of threat, this was possibly the safest place to leave her.

Whereas she, Marilyn, could exit as easy as pushing a button.

She looked up to see Trudy staring at her from the bottom step of the porch.

"My goodness!" said Marilyn. "How long have you been there?"

"It's horrible, being without your senses, isn't it?" Trudy said. "Come on, I found your spot."

* * *

MARILYN EMERGED ON BODECKER BOULEVARDE, behind an empty bus stop. A sign on the bus shelter showed the date and the weather forecast. It was the evening of four nights before the letter had arrived at the Office of Dead Letters, and she was in for some light rain.

She closed her eyes and breathed in deeply. All around her was the noise of the City as its people hurried home or strolled out to dinner and a show. The sound was a mishmash of chaos and order, the brakes of cars and omnibuses, the braying of horses, raised voices and laughter, a hawker selling newspapers, a street girl sweeping the footpath, and oh! All those wonderful hearts beating, beating, some fast, some slow, and their breath coming and going and their feet shuffling hither and thither like a dance.

It was all so very beautiful.

Marilyn opened her eyes. She bought a newspaper and gave the street sweeper her change. She snapped her purse shut and smiled at the sound it made.

Her own home was currently occupied by her past self, so she had to find somewhere to spend the next few nights. Marilyn thought of that other Marilyn, currently at home cooking a fish stew, soon to curl up on the sofa with a book. She suddenly realised that she couldn't remember the last time she had eaten. Was it the night before in Megal's den when they had had Sino food? That was an eternity ago.

Marilyn rarely went out into the City at night. She had embraced the quiet domesticity that the Office of Dead Letters had enabled. She had enjoyed her brief walk to the office and maintaining the fiction of being a homebody with a penchant for opening letters. She even enjoyed the inane small talk with Trudy, she realised. But she'd always had the niggling feeling that the peaceful life was only ever temporary. She'd had no idea then what life after the letters would look like and she seemed to have less idea now.

On the corner was an all-night diner of the sort that she and her sister used to go to before her sister had dropped out of college. Marilyn went in and ordered the dish of the day and flicked through the evening newspaper. Funny to think that this hot-off-the-press edition was already old news. If she'd have known she was coming back, she could have memorised the lottery numbers and told her present self! Marilyn smiled. She wasn't that sort of person.

When the waitress arrived with the menu, Marilyn asked her if there was a post office nearby.

"Oh, naw love, it wouldn't be open now like," the waitress said.

"No," Marilyn agreed. "But for tomorrow?"

"I tell you what, though, Mr Jimmy's got some stamps out the back. We could sell you one of those, right, and then you can just drop it in a box."

"What time is the mail picked up, do you know?" Marilyn asked.

"Oh, aye, I think the box on the corner is at midnight. Mr Charlie! Is that right? Midnight for the post box?"

"Eleven minutes before," called back the chef.

"There you go. How's that for punctuality? Gotta love the postal service," said the waitress with a large smile.

"You do," said Marilyn. "You really do."

She glanced at the clock on the wall. She had 43 minutes until the mail was picked up. If she didn't post the letter, none of this would happen, she thought. 12 Jellicoe Street wouldn't disappear, and Trudy wouldn't create the anomaly. She could live her life peacefully and never, ever have to go to that world of nothingness.

But there was already another Marilyn here. Was Overworld big enough for two Marilyns? She smiled at the thought.

She had no desire to go back and prevent the wars. She didn't want to get involved in espionage, or fight on a battlefield. She didn't want to slay any Underworlders, or lay any traps, or destroy any bridges. But there were other things she could fix. Small things that could make a big difference. She had this extraordinary power; she could actually help people.

Well, in any case, she had time to enjoy a hot dish of apple-roasted beef, and damn if she wasn't going to. She even agreed to a chocolate and banana cupcake when the waitress suggested it.

Marilyn looked out the window of the diner. The glass was speckled with raindrops, and she could see the distorted lights of the occasional car that swooshed past on the slick road. She ate the beef and thought of Trudy stuck there in that nowhere place with no food, no drinks, no sound, no nothing. She wondered again what Trudy's skill was, what enhanced senses she had – and what she was living without.

She could just not send the letter…

"Here you are love," said the waitress and put a small plate with a cupcake on it in front of Marilyn. "And here's your stamp, too, if you're still wanting it."

"That's very kind," said Marilyn automatically. She looked at the stamp. It was a *baccillus fungiatus*. It was from the mushroom collection of the autumn before last.

"When did you get this?" Marilyn asked the waitress, who was already halfway back to the kitchen. "Excuse me, miss, do you know when you bought this stamp?"

"Oh Mister Jimmy probably got those years ago. Rarely uses em, really. Just likes to have them around, just in case. Never know when you might need a stamp."

Marilyn finished up her cupcake with a smile. Well, that settled that. The universe seemed to be telling her what to do and she was never one to disobey orders.

"All done then?" said the waitress.

"Yes, it was delicious, thank you," Marilyn said. "I say, could you help me? My hands are greasy from the cupcake. Do you think you could write the address on the envelope for me?"

"Sure, love, pleasure. Hardly get to send letters meself, since my son got the receiver put in. Not really the same though, is it?" said the waitress. "Where's it going to then?"

"12 Jellicoe Street," Marilyn said.

The waitress smiled. "Oh, that's just a few streets away from where me old people live. Small world, hey?"

"Sometimes it feels like it's getting smaller," Marilyn said.

21

The regiment of dead letters

Yes, sometimes the world felt very small indeed, thought Marilyn, as she stepped out of 13 Jellicoe Street. She crossed the road to where an unlikely gaggle of people were peering at a spot on an unremarkable looking fence.

"You let it go!" Megal was yelling at Isabel. "Why the damn hell did you close it?"

"I say," Dr Simon said, stepping forward. Megal rounded on him, his face red and blotchy.

"What is it exactly that you object to, Doctor?" He spat the last word out as though it had a bad taste. Simon looked at his employer, his eyebrows raised.

"You know exactly what I object to," he said, quietly. "Your behaviour is unseemly."

"A word you wouldn't be able to find in a dictionary," Megal said.

"Hello," Marilyn said. "What's this about then?"

"Marilyn!" Isabel yelled, and threw herself at her in a great hug. "You're here. You're now! But I just saw you!" She turned and pointed at the fence, switching her gaze between it and Marilyn several times.

"That was four days ago," Marilyn said, pulling herself back and smoothing down her dress. "I'm here now."

"But where have you been?"

Marilyn looked over her shoulder.

"At number 13," she said.

"What!" said Isabel. "With the eyeless lady?"

"Hm," said Marilyn. It had not been a comfortable place to spend the past few days. She had survived on tea and biscuits, listening to the rantings of the eyeless woman, until she had left with the other Marilyn that morning.

"That's why I couldn't smell you!" said Isabel.

"So it would appear," said Marilyn. She suddenly smiled, her whole face beaming. "It's so very good to see you all again."

"Miss Marilyn," said Dr Simon, stepping forward. "You are truly a magnificent woman! To have not only found your way in to the anomaly, but to have made your way out and be standing here before us…" He dropped his head and seemed to wipe a tear from his eye.

"It's all right, Doctor Simon," Marilyn said. "We all did our best."

"Damn tooting," said Isabel.

"The Office of Dead Letters achieved its purpose and we are all here," said Marilyn. "Dr Simon, how long will the anomaly remain stable here? Miss Trudy thinks that she is acting as a sort of anchor, keeping it in place."

"I believe she is right," said Dr Simon. "And the longer she stays inside, the further back in time the anomaly will stretch. Perhaps one day 12 Jellicoe Street will never have existed at all!" He grinned widely and Marilyn couldn't help but smile back at him. His skill was misdirected enthusiasm, she realised.

"I would very much like to talk to Miss Trudy," Megal said. "Is there any way of getting inside again? Or is it cut off to us now? And indeed, how did you get out?"

"I think when Miss Trudy is ready, she'll come and find you," she said to Megal.

"Well," the doctor said. "Miss Marilyn. Allow me to

congratulate you for having the power to move between worlds. Not just the Two Worlds, but all of them."

He took her hands between his own. Marilyn had forgotten to put on her gloves and she felt the full force of his skin against her own. After days of nothing but beige and then locked away at number 13 with the old lady, her sense of feeling was starved, and she was struck fiercely by the contact. She felt every iota of Dr Simon's genuine congratulations – and everything that lay underneath. The tremendous force made her catch her breath and pull back. She looked up into his eyes, heard the cadence of his breath, and then she leaned in close to his ear.

"Oh, Dr Simon, you are not a failure. Here we all are. I have travelled through space and time thanks to you," she said. She looked at him again, and saw that there actually were tears in his eyes.

"Thank you," he said quietly.

Marilyn reached inside her satchel and put her gloves back on before stepping to face Megal. She took his hands.

"Don't be angry with anyone," she said. "That's how wars begin."

Megal smiled at her and looked significantly at her gloves.

"So…" he said. "You fear touching me?"

"I think I know what I'll find," she said.

Megal smiled ruefully but said nothing

Marilyn withdrew her hands and turned to face them all. She had spent the past few days wondering how much she would share with them, how much she could trust them. Now was time to find out.

"General of the First Order Trudy Grayling has sacrificed herself by staying within the anomaly," she said. "She believes she can stop wars before they happen. I believe she's right."

Marilyn closed her eyes and reached out her hand. She felt the entry point to the anomaly and pushed against it, gently, so gently, and heard her comrades gasp to see the space begin to open. She opened her eyes and closed the gap again.

"I can go back and forth as I please," Marilyn said. "We can stop things in the past. We can help people."

Megal stared at her. "What do you mean? Just go back and stop the wars from happening? But that will change everything. We may not even exist."

"Basic space time error, Mr Megal," Marilyn said with a smile.

"Indeed," said Dr Simon. "Well, I would be honoured to serve with you on this mission, Miss Marilyn."

"Don't be ridiculous," Isabel said. "Men can't enlist! You know that I'm 100% in, Miss Marilyn."

"As am I," said Helena, who was standing nearby.

"Thank you, ladies," said Marilyn. "Gentlemen, it may be that we will need to call upon you to serve Overworld. In the meantime, enlistees, may I welcome you to the Regiment of Dead Letters."

Afterword

The Office of Dead Letters began as a phrase, then with an unshakeable image of two women sitting at a desk, covered in paper dust, opening letters. Once I entered that room with them, I simply followed where they went.

I hope you have enjoyed following them, too.

xNat

First Chapter Preview

Take a sneak peak at the first chapter of the second book in the Two Worlds series The Door of Inconvenience. *You'll meet new heroes and learn about the mysterious Underworld - and there's plenty more of Marilyn, Isabel and Dr Simon, too.*

The leather making street in Encyc stunk of human piss and animal suffering. The smell wafted through the laneways, wormed its way into the woodwork, wriggled under windows, and streamed through vents and gutters. People had long ago given up stoppering the gaps in their homes and shops; the smell always got in, and once in it never got out.

Agnetha Moon walked down the street with her hands in the pockets of her leather trousers, eyes straight ahead. She had a slouch to her shoulders that the other pedestrians recognised, and nobody stopped her to say hello or ask a favour or offer her a tidbit of information. When Agnetha had her swagger on, nobody was stupid enough to get in her way.

Well, almost nobody.

"Miss Aggie! Miss Aggie! Wait up, would you?" A girl, no more than 125 centimetres of her, ran behind Agnetha, but her little legs were no match for Agnetha's stroll. "Don't you hear me? Wait, I said! I've got something you want to hear."

Agnetha stopped in her tracks and turned on her heel very slowly to face the bundle running towards her. She dug her hands a little further into her pockets, rounded her shoulders a little more. A leather seller out sweeping his stoop took one look at her and retreated into the safety of his smelly atelier.

"Miss Maisie Brown, this better be good," Agnetha growled down at the urchin. Maisie was bent over, panting, and when she looked up she had sweat beading on her brow.

"Yes, Miss Aggie. You know I only ever have the best information for you."

"Not here, you fool. Come on."

Agnetha kept her hands in her pockets but straightened her slouch a little. And she deigned to slow down so that the girl could move at a brisk walk and didn't need to run to keep up.

"You sure do walk fast, Miss Aggie."

"Well, I'm a busy lady, Miss Maisie."

The girl beamed up at her. "I like that you call me Miss, even though I'm only little still."

"You'll be big enough soon enough," said Agnetha. "May as well get used to this cruel world."

They carried on in silence, except for the sound of Maisie panting, until they reached a dingy cottage. Agnetha took her hands out of her pockets and unlocked the door, ushering the little girl inside the dark hallway.

"You know the rules," she said, tossing the keys into a dish on the hall table. "Don't touch anything, don't see anything, don't smell anything, don't know anything."

They walked past a series of closed doors to the kitchen out the back, which afforded a stunning view of a weedy courtyard and a sooty brick wall. Agnetha poured the girl a glass of apple juice and cracked open a beer for herself, flicking the bottle cap behind the back door where it joined hundreds of others.

"Spill it."

Maisie was a good kid, but annoying. She kept her eyes open. Unfortunately, she often kept her mouth open, too, and Agnetha didn't trust blabbermouths. Occasionally she'd brought an interesting bit of information – all the street kids were keen to get in Ag's good books – but mostly she dealt in trivia and gossip.

"Wesley Barbarino's house has got a door into Underworld," Maisie said.

Agnetha swallowed her swig of beer and put the bottle down on the bench behind her.

"Say that again," she said.

Maisie repeated herself, oblivious to the iciness of Agnetha's tone.

"Where'd you get your intel from?"

"We were playing at Wesley's house and the ball rolled down into the basement. I saw it myself," Maisie said. She was sitting on the bench opposite Agnetha, kicking the doors with her heels. "Say, can I get another glass of juice?"

Agnetha breathed out loudly and almost laughed. "You saw a door in a basement? Is that all? Kid, you need better material. You're lucky I'm feeling generous or I'd add you to my collection downstairs."

Maisie made a horrified look. "You wouldn't do that to a kid!" she said. "Besides, look how little I am! You'd barely make a few dollars."

"I don't know," said Agnetha, with a wicked grin. "You got that fat belly and those fat little legs."

Maisie jumped down from the bench and glared up at Ag. "Oh, if you're going to be rude, I'll just take my information elsewhere. Somewhere it will be valued."

"You don't have any information," Ag said, and she skulled the rest of her beer. "You've got a door. That's all. Every basement in Encyc has a door."

"I saw it," Maisie said. "I saw it open. I saw green on the other side. I saw hills like what we don't have here in Encyc. I saw flowers and fields. And I saw a tall white man with long silver hair, walking with a cane made of gold."

"Plenty of tall white men around here. Nothing special about that," Agnetha said.

"Oh!" said Maisie, stamping her foot. "Why won't you believe me? I know what I saw. Yeah, I know I'm too young to remember Underworld, but I know I saw something that I've never seen before, something that doesn't exist on Overworld. Why don't you believe me?"

Maisie was at the point of anger that could easily blub over into tears, and Agnetha couldn't bear the idea of tears.

"Okay, kid. I believe you. I do. Anyone who sees Underworld knows it. I believe you."

"Then why are you being so mean to me?"

Agnetha looked down at the angry little face before her. Angry little girl, like she had been, like she still was, although she was tall as the moon now.

"Life is tough, kid," Agnetha said. "And I'm tougher. You want to be tough, too? Or do you want to blubber?"

"I never blubber," Maisie said fiercely.

Agnetha fished out a coin from the depths of her pockets and flicked it over to the girl.

"All right, scram. And thanks for the intel. I appreciate it." Maisie caught the coin with one hand and tucked it into her overalls. She started to walk back to the dark hall and the front door. "And don't you tell anybody else!" Ag yelled after her.

"Make it worth my while," said Maisie. "I'll give you 24 hours."

Agnetha grinned, in spite of herself. Smart kid, she thought. Dumb smart kid.

But the intel, if it were true, was deadly serious. Doors to Underworld were her domain, and if the Barbarinos had found one without telling her, they would have to answer some very pointy questions.

She finished her beer, checked the knives under her jacket, and went to pay the Barbarinos a visit.

About the Author

Nat Newman is an award-winning writer whose short stories have appeared in journals such as Granta, Structo, Brittle Star and Shoreline of Infinity. In 2017, she won the Commonwealth Short Story Prize for the Pacific Region with her story "The Death of Margaret Roe".

Born and raised in Australia, Nat has walked across two countries, lived and worked in six, and now calls the universe her home. When she's not dreaming up new worlds for readers to enjoy, she runs an animal shelter in the Philippines. *The Office of Dead Letters* is her first novella.

Liked this book? Why not review it on Amazon or Goodreads?

You can connect with me at:
https://www.natnewman.com
https://twitter.com/@lividlili
https://www.facebook.com/natnewmanwriter

Subscribe to my newsletter:
http://eepurl.com/hkfs-r

www.ingramcontent.com/pod-product-compliance
Lightning Source LLC
Chambersburg PA
CBHW070340130626
46556CB00007B/2954